W9-CEW-153

IN THE
SNOW FOREST

ALSO BY ROY PARVIN

The Loneliest Road in America

IN THE
SNOW FOREST

Three Novellas

ROY PARVIN

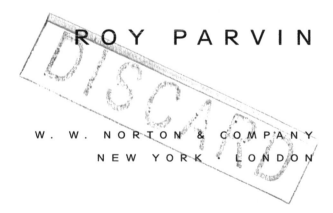

W. W. NORTON & COMPANY
NEW YORK   LONDON

For information about permission to reproduce selections from this book, write to
Permissions, W. W. Norton & Company, 500 Fifth Avenue, New York, NY 10110

The text of this book is composed in Bembo, with the display set in Spartan

Composition by Thomas Ernst

Manufacturing by Maple-Vail Book Manufacturing Group

Book design by BTDnyc

LIBRARY OF CONGRESS CATALOGING-IN-PUBLICATION DATA

Parvin, Roy.
    In the snow forest : three novellas / Roy Parvin.
        p.   cm.
    Contents: Betty Hutton—In the snow forest—Menno's granddaughter.
    ISBN 0-393-04977-9
    1. Trinity Alps Region (Calif.)—Social life and customs—Fiction. 2. California,
Northern—Social life and customs—Fiction. I. Title.
PS3566.A7726 I5 2000
813.'54—dc21   00-034868

W. W. Norton & Company, Inc., 500 Fifth Avenue, New York, N.Y. 10110
www.wwnorton.com

W. W. Norton & Company Ltd., 10 Coptic Street, London WC1A 1PU

2 3 4 5 6 7 8 9 0

TO *Janet*

AND *Carol Houck Smith*

AND *my mother, who has always told me stories*

CONTENTS

Weather, snowing and blowing same as yesterday. We are in a very weak state, but we cannot give in. We often talk about poor Captain Scott and the blizzard that finished him and party. If we had stayed in our tent another day I don't think we should have got under way at all, and we should have shared the same fate. But if the worst comes we have made up our minds to carry on and die in harness.

—SIR ERNEST SHACKLETON, *South,*
diary entry, February 25, 1916

BETTY HUTTON

He was a big man who looked like trouble, even with his glasses. A cruel fact of nature that made Gibbs a prisoner of his own body long before he became an actual one, at Pine River or the various and lesser security county facilities before that.

He'd been back in the world for months now and had few things to show for it, chiefly a girlfriend and a parole officer, neither of whom was able to give Gibbs what he really needed or wanted, and, truth be told, Gibbs himself hadn't the clearest idea of what that might be either.

"I guess I'm waiting for opportunity to suggest itself to me," he'd explained to his parole bull. "I think it's one of those little-birdy-will-tell-me type situations."

"A birdy," O'Donoghue echoed, a stick of a man with a third-act sort of look to him. "Now I've heard it all. I guess a birdy beats grifting antiques, though."

"I'm not thinking a bird is going to actually speak to me," Gibbs had said. "Unless it's a parakeet or something." He was not stupid, though it often seemed the world was telling him otherwise. All he knew about was old things or how to make a thing look old. During his last bit in the can he'd seen killing, and what struck him about it was how easy it was. Anybody could do it.

From the deck of Jolie's second-story apartment he could glimpse the Atlantic, if he craned his head, perching on tiptoes. It was October of 1975, the year beginning to die more than just a little, the Jersey shoretown of Barnegat Light wearing the season like a down-at-the-heels beauty queen, the summer crowds vacating after Labor Day, neon glaze of the arcades finally switched off, revealing a pitted sweep of beach with all the charm and color of dirty concrete, the slack Atlantic crawling ashore, a pocket watch winding down.

But it was what stood at his back, the ocean of land behind Gibbs, that pulled at him like a tide. He'd never been farther west than the eastern fringe of Pennsylvania, had never been anywhere. He'd heard about Montana, though, a place that sounded like everything hadn't yet been decided, where there still might be some time left. A cellmate had told him of the chinooks, the southerly winds capable of turning winter into spring in a matter of hours, sometimes a ninety-degree temperature swing, and it had seemed to Gibbs lying in their dank cement crib, it seemed if such a thing as the chinooks was possible, anything was.

It was a sandblasted fall morning that he happened on the Chrysler, a rust-scabbed Newport parked along a dead end of bungalows clapped shut for the season, the car blue and about the size of a narwhal, its white vinyl roof gone to peel, a whip antenna for a CB the car no longer owned. It looked like the beginning to a thought that Gibbs couldn't see his way to the end of.

As he stared at the car, two things came to mind. That Jolie had been hiding her squirrel's stash of mad money in a coffee can on a high kitchen shelf. And the practical knowledge gleaned from his time at the wall of how to jack an automobile, which indeed proved easy enough, a matter of popping the door, taking a screwdriver to the steering column, touching off the appropriate wires, and then, like some low-grade miracle, the car rattling awake, exhaling an extravagant tail of blue smoke.

That was how it started: with two wrongs. After a lifetime of wrongs, what were two more? Nothing, Gibbs told himself, nothing. It was just possible he'd finally stumbled on the two wrongs that actually might produce a right.

He didn't take much with him: a leather satchel swollen with a few changes of clothes, his shaving kit, sundry effects; a paper sack of sham works: jades and Roman carnelians and openwork medallions; and, shoved between both on the backseat, an antique pistol, a keepsake handed down in his family, more a piece of history than an actual piece, the only article of legitimate value among the lot. Out the back window, Barnegat Light framed like a diminishing postcard. That was where trouble would come from when it did, from behind. He tugged on the rearview mirror, yanked it free from its mooring, and then there was only the gray road ahead.

A tattered map inside the Chrysler's glove box ran as far as Harrisburg. After that, Gibbs imagined himself, past the banks of the Susquehanna, falling out the other side of the country, running free, into territory unbound by state lines or the iron sway of laws.

He drove clear around the circle of hours, until all the license plates on the road read Wisconsin. Gibbs pulled off to refuel, him running on fumes as much as the car. A gas jockey shaped like a butterball stepped out of the office and Gibbs stood to stretch his legs, to take measure on the endless table of land fleeing to every point of horizon. At the far corner of the lot, tethered to a pole, was the strangest animal he'd ever seen, looked like he didn't know what, devil eyes set high on its head.

Gibbs said, "What kind of dog is that?"

"It's a goat," the gas jockey told him.

Gibbs nodded heavily. "I didn't think it was a dog."

"Michigan," the jockey said and it took Gibbs a few beats to catch his meaning and then he remembered swapping plates the evening before at a reststop outside Franklin, Pennsylvania, with a listing Travelall bearing Michigan tags.

"Yeah, the Lions and Tigers. Motor City."

The jockey asked what he wanted, couldn't have been any more than seventeen, all pimples and baby fat. Over his heart: *Hank* stitched in script. Gibbs glanced around for anybody else and there was no one. Back at Pine River, a whole class of inmate specialized in burgling gas stations, called it *striking oil.*

"What do I want," Gibbs laughed. "Well, Hank, I want it all."

"I meant gas."

"Right. Good man. Fill it with regular. Knock yourself out."

Hank propped the hood. On the pump, the scratchy spinning of the gallon dial. The roll of money that Gibbs had filched from Jolie bulged the pocket of his trousers, the size of a baby's fist. He sized up the goat as it grazed leggy plants in a flower box.

And then a strange thing.

It was as if the person who was Gibbs vanished altogether and he could see the entire scene like it was in front of him, a big man standing in the filling bay, a teenager under the hood of a car wiping the dipstick with a rag, the numbing horizontal of land on all sides. And he watched to see what the big man would do, waiting for the squeal of the hood's hinges as it dropped, the blackjack crunch of it slamming the jockey on the crown of his head, laying him out on the oil-splotched concrete, peaceful as an afternoon nap.

It was the pump boy's hand reaching over the lip of the hood that brought Gibbs back to the there and then, the hood gently closing, Hank leaning on it till the catch held fast. Gibbs stared off at a windbreak of buckeye chestnuts, his heart throttling, the dry rattle of the few leaves still on the branches.

Hank pulled a part from a pocket, massaged it with a rag as if trying to screw it into his palm. "You're missing a rearview mirror, you know."

Gibbs said, "I've seen enough of what's behind me."

Nothing left to do but pay. He was spooked yet. Hank appeared none the wiser, doling out change slowly, making sure to get it right.

Gibbs folded himself into the Chrysler. In a few moments he'd be back on his way. For the time being, though, all he was was afraid. A close call, he told himself. Easing out the filling bay, he rolled down the window. "It's a funny world, Hank," he said, pointing at the goat. "Things aren't always what they seem. You know the one about wooden nickels, don't you?"

"Yes sir."

"Good man."

TWO DAYS LATER and it was Montana.

Thus far it wasn't entirely what Gibbs had expected. The sky was indeed big and everywhere. But Hokanson, his cellmate from Pine River, had mentioned mountains. He'd told about mining, too, the strikes of gold and silver. "An occupation," Hokanson had promised, "where nothing's required other than doggedness and luck." Gibbs had liked the sound of that.

For a distance of miles the road banded the tracks of the Great Northern and he raced a train with a string of cars long enough almost to be considered geography. There were no posted speed limits, so Gibbs could open the Chrysler up.

He drew a high line through the eastern end of the state, through flat prairie grasslands and fields already disked for winter wheat, through one-horse towns so small they hardly rated as towns at all, a grain elevator at the outskirts, then a short business strip, usually a grange hall and a church or two and a cross-hatching of streets off the main, the neat rows of side-gabled houses at the edge of the frontier.

It was not until after Devon had spread across the front windshield and out the back, after Ethridge and Cut Bank had come and gone, not until Blackfoot that he saw the mountains.

They rose before him, out of the west and yellowed plain like a wave, and Gibbs drove toward them, his anticipation gathering like a wave itself.

He made Glacier as the sun was emptying from the sky. The calendar still said October though it felt later than that now, the mountaintops webbed in snow, switchbacked roads cut high onto the white shoulders, as if with pinking shears. A different world from the one he'd left behind: wilder and somehow older.

It was late enough in both the day and season that the guard at the gate to Glacier just waved him through, and Gibbs wheeled the Chrysler down a park road lined with the tall green of Engelmann spruce and Doug fir, pulling up at a lake a couple miles on.

It was lovely—he had no other words to match up with the landscape—only lovely and cold. The lake looked even colder yet and it stretched out before him glassy as a marble, the smudge of twilight already descending, the surround of mountains holding a few clouds within their spires like a cage. A solitary bird flew low over the water, the lake reflecting sky and bird so that it looked like two birds on the wing. Off in the distance, he could see the road following the contours of the shore.

In the foreground: a beach of fine pebbles, a woman and a little kid seated at water's edge. Gibbs couldn't remember his last real conversation that hadn't concerned gas or lodging, and with the day guttering like a candle all he wanted right now was to share the moment with someone, an exchange of pleasantries that he associated with regular life.

He skimmed through what he had to say for himself. So many places and things in the last few days, the mad rush out, but all the hours and miles of driving bled in a dreamy smear now.

The kid didn't look more than a year and change, just a tyke scooping handfuls of stones, flinging them into the shallows with both arms, exclaiming a pleased trill of gibberish with each throw.

"He has all the earmarks of a major leaguer," Gibbs said, coming up from behind.

The woman started as if a gun had been fired over her shoulder.

Gibbs smiled at her as harmlessly as he could, showing his impossible teeth, wideset as tombstones in a cemetery. "Just look at him," he said softer, indicating the boy, "throwing with either arm, swinging from both sides of the windmill."

The woman regarded Gibbs, a shielding hand over her eyes to block the last light, like an explorer gazing off into a great distance. Her surprise resettled into a pleasant face, her hair not blond or red but falling somewhere in between, the kid's coloring pretty much the same and it suited them both. Gibbs figured she was younger than him, though not by a lot, a bit late for family rearing. That was how it was done these days, sometimes not even a man in the picture, which could have been the case here.

"I never know what to call them at that age," he said. "Babies or toddlers."

"Elliot," the woman said and smiled herself.

The kid held up another handful of rocks. Gibbs winked and the boy tossed them, pockmarking the skin of water.

"A handsome little man," Gibbs told her. "A crackerjack. I'm sure you get tired of hearing that."

"Oh, I don't think so," the woman said.

"No, I wouldn't think so either," Gibbs said. He liked her smile, how it closed the space between them, held nothing back, no room for anything but it. It made him feel more than who he was.

A diving platform a hundred yards off bobbed and slapped at the water, the far rim of the lake now more an idea than a physical thing.

"They say you can see two hundred miles," the woman said. "On a clear day. That's hard to believe."

"That's something," Gibbs agreed. "Two hundred miles."

"I read it in a brochure."

"Well, then it must be true."

In rapid strokes the day dimmed, clouds blacking out, pin-prick of stars here and there. The wind kicked up a chop on the lake, like pulled stitching. Gibbs watched the woman button the kid against the evening chill, the coat ill-fitting, perhaps a hand-me-down or from the church donation bin. The kid squirmed worse than an eel, wanting no part of it, wanting only the rocks. The woman persisted as if nothing was more important than this, than making sure the kid was warm, her face tired yet burnished with devotion, a face that said to Gibbs that things might not have been the easiest but if she got this simple task right, then maybe life might tell a different story for the boy, a hope that attached to her like a shine.

Gibbs felt he was spying on them. He drifted back to the car, sat behind the big circle of steering wheel. In the dark, the woman's face stayed with him. A raven flapped over the windshield, like a hinged W; across the way, twin pearls of headlights throwing cables into the black. Gibbs would have bet down to the green felt of the table that the boy was an accident, all she had to show for bad times and worse memories.

There was still her hope, so much it seemed to extend to Gibbs as well. She could have gathered up the kid back there, turned tail, the daily papers full of accounts of what could happen to a woman and a child alone in the night. A face that held that much trust—Gibbs would have stolen another auto, driven another nineteen hundred miles just to look into another such face.

He reached for the paper sack on the backseat, withdrew a jade piece he could identify by touch alone, stood out from the car and double-timed back to the lakeshore, fearing the woman and Elliot might have moved on, but they were still there, turning to Gibbs as he approached, as if waiting.

He bent to show what was in his hand, told about the fish, which was green and long and slender, fashioned with incised fins and a squared mouth. "From the Shang dynasty," he said. "It dates back to well over a thousand years before Jesus. Something this ancient—in its own way, it's a lot like seeing two hundred miles, isn't it?" Gibbs was tempted to hand the jade over to the boy but thought the better of it because it just might wind up in the drink and gave it to the woman instead.

She turned it with a careful finger. "It's pretty," she said and it was. In some circles it wouldn't amount to more than a passable imitation, but it was still pretty; he'd even gone to the trouble of filing an edge off one corner of the tail. By his lights, all that should be worth something.

"For the boy's college fund," Gibbs explained. He'd not see her after tonight, would never see her again, but maybe they'd remember him for that.

The woman switched her gaze from the jade to him.

"How do you like that, bub," Gibbs said, poking the boy in his tight round of belly. The kid ducked behind the woman, peeked out.

"I'm Claire," she said.

"Gibbs," he told her. "My name's Gibbs."

He thought she'd beg it off, a gift from a stranger, but she curled her hand around the jade, shook it like dice. She swept her other arm back behind her to bring the boy forward. "Look at this, Elliot," she said, then studied Gibbs, a face like a question. "Well, we thank you, Mr. Gibbs."

"No, it's just Gibbs," he said. "There's no mister about it."

IT WAS FULL NIGHT when he quit Glacier. The road wound amidst close hills and, high above, points of stars flashed. He had everywhere and nowhere to go.

He thought the random thoughts of a man behind the

wheel of a car. He considered his kid brother, hadn't in the longest time and now he did. Miles was a scientist who researched genes. The last time Gibbs had seen him was the old man's funeral, before Pine River. After the burial, Miles had talked about his work, the fact of DNA carrying the code of a person's makeup, down to the soul practically. Gibbs followed the spiral of explanation the best he could, nodding like a woodpecker, until all the talk of markers sounded only like poker. Miles grew increasingly fidgety and Gibbs had wondered if maybe there wasn't something else his brother was trying to tell him. In the end Miles had said maybe it wasn't such a good idea for Gibbs to contact him for a while, his forehead crumpling like paper. "It's just that I have a wife now and there's the kids," he said, leaving the thought unfinished, for it to spin in the air between them like flies. "It's okay, Miles," Gibbs had assured him. "If I were related to me I wouldn't want to know me either. No harm, no foul."

As it turned out, it'd been like mourning two deaths for Gibbs, that of the old man and Miles, too. And he was the only one left.

There'd been Hokanson, the sole opportunity for fraternity that custody had afforded. Hokanson was a nasty piece of work, a transfer from a distant facility out west, his crimes so monstrous that he was remanded thousands of miles back to the tidal flats of Jersey for his own safety. None of the other numbers could say exactly what he'd done, only talk, but even the hardest cases swung wide of him.

Hokanson and Gibbs, though, had got on without incident. After lights-out, he'd tell Gibbs stories of Montana, that eerie, raspy voice, almost like metal-on-metal, the trail of words leading into the nameless hours.

The facility at Pine River was erected on marshy land, hard by the steady rustle of the Atlantic. On nights of particular full moons the water table rose, the floor of their matchbox quarters awash in brine, and on those nights Hokanson's words were of unique comfort. As long as he talked, that barred world went away, the murmurings down the cellblock row of dangerous men crying and praying and talking in their sleep, the stories sticking with Gibbs long after Hokanson had gone, tales of a place big enough that there still might be room for someone like him.

HE STAYED THAT NIGHT outside Glacier in a town called Hungry Horse, in an efficiency unit at a motel, a room with mismatched burners on the gas stove and a stale ammonia odor, like a convalescent home. Gibbs suspected he was the only guest for the evening but later heard a car trunk slam and the scrabble of a key finding the lock, then the door to the next room swinging open on creaky hinges. A woman's throaty voice carried through the shared wall. "You *already* told me more than I want to know," it said and then a deeper voice answering, unintelligible, little more than a grunt.

Gibbs woke during the middle of the night to a train whistle. A picture came to mind, an old-timey locomotive chug-chugging through the pleats of hill, a plume of smoke mingling with the feathering evergreens, a soothing image.

Sleep seemed like another place he'd left behind. There was a light outside the curtained window, the moon, the same moon shining over the shoretown in Jersey he'd fled although it didn't feel that way. He mulled over what he knew about motels, how they were largely a charge card business these days, whatever cash on hand probably secured in a strongbox. And he could sense the impulses edging in, as familiar and thick as blood, and he tried to think of something else. He thought about the Claire woman from earlier, from the lake, how her hope seemed to flow as easy as instinct, as easy as breathing, a gift. Gibbs would have given almost anything for such hope. Years before, he'd forsaken drink and at the time it'd seemed like the hardest thing in the world but he now understood it wasn't.

A dog barked out on the road and down the way another answered it, back and forth, and he could imagine the chorus being picked up in houses further down the line, the call and response carrying all through Montana, as long as the road stretched, and he suddenly felt far away from anything he'd ever known. Gibbs dropped into sleep, picturing again a locomotive, a mare's tail of smoke over a steel trestle bridge and a bottom-less gorge below, the warm sensation that he was arriving at some destination but wasn't quite there yet.

FOR THE NEXT FEW DAYS, Gibbs was content to stay put, operating without purpose, letting the hours assume their own shape. He had money in his pocket and he put up in motels and ate as if he'd the key to the king's larder.

He whiled away an afternoon in Kalispell watching planes wing in to the airport. In Whitefish he found a park with a lake that was not as big or majestic as the lake in Glacier, and along the rocky beach, a canoe. Nobody was around and Gibbs paddled out.

An overcast day, gray mountains ringing the horizon and merging with sky, the lakeshore vacation homes perched on stilty legs, dark and empty. From experience he knew one couldn't count on finding anything of value in such places but you never really knew—sometimes you got lucky. Gibbs considered the steep A-frames like possibilities, then paddled back.

Happy hour: sounds of drinking, lively discussion about if it might snow wafting out of the avenue bars. He walked to the end of town, suppertime in the boxy hall-and-parlor houses. He watched in the dark as he would a TV with the sound off, tried to envision himself inside among them.

He used to taunt his prey, in the prickly moments before hands got thrown, used to ask, "Do you know physics? Do you know what happens when an object comes up against an immovable object?" To a man they'd been more chump than victim, would have done the same to him if they could have— that was what he told himself then, what he repeated now. And he watched the cheery scenes on the other side of glass, brothers and sisters passing servings around kitchen tables, Gibbs taking it in like something he needed, almost like food.

. . .

SO FAR IT'D ALL BEEN fine and good, but Gibbs had no further clue about that place that might have him.

He drove north one morning, the road following the river which fattened into a reservoir, at one end a dam straddling the shores like a giant ship. He crossed a bridge to the other side, the road snaking in the green of fir and spruce, turning into a hill, a bit of snow skiffed in some places, then more, then everything coated, the evidence of a recent plow, the oil-and-gravel surface still navigable.

Gibbs hadn't encountered another vehicle since gaining the woods. He wondered how close he was to Canada. At the crest of hill, a pocket alpine lake iced over and in the middle of it, a plywood shanty. Woodsmoke pulled out a stack on the top and a pair of window squares were glazed in mist, a tiny house on the ice. He'd never seen a house on the ice before.

He wasn't prepared for the chill outside the Chrysler, which struck like a hammer. He rapped on the door, heard a shuffling inside, then the door opening, a blocky, lumpish fellow in gumboots and nylon pants blinking up, a pile of white hair on his head like a tornado funnel. Behind, a lantern glowed. Gibbs could not get over the tidy cubby—wood benches on opposite walls, shelves all around, a little hinged table that dropped down, a kerosene heater, the floor covered in board except for a few circles cut away to expose the ice below.

"Shoot, fella, you gave old Ernest here quite a scare," the

man said. "Thought you might be the missus. I'm taking me one of those mental health days."

Gibbs explained himself the best he could.

"Jesus, man. You must be catching the death of it." Ernest stepped back to admit Gibbs into the shanty. "So you never been hard-water fishing is what you're telling me."

Gibbs allowed that he'd not.

"Then you're in for a treat. Gibbs you said it was? A name you don't hear every day. I suppose that's your business." He looked over Gibbs, then handed him a spoon auger, demonstrating how to bore into the ice. "You're a big enough man to handle it yourself. Good Lord, look at your feet. Must make buying shoes a trial. You know what they say about big feet, don't you. Big feet, big shoes. You can tell me to shut up any time."

He outfitted Gibbs with a tip-up equipped with a bell that jingled when a fish was on the take. Ernest managed a jig pole, a rod so small it looked like gear for a pygmy. He told Gibbs about himself, blinking rapidly the whole time, about his panel truck, how he hauled trash for a number of the homes dotting these hills. Winters he fit a blade on the front end and did some plowing. "A lazy man who's always had the curse of having to work hard. Married twice. First time was poison, the second, the cure. Wife number one accused me of being Ernest in earnest, and vice versa."

Gibbs smiled. "I bet you are."

A whiff of kerosene hung in the interior. Ernest cracked a window, air entering like a knife but still cozy in the ice bob.

Gibbs realized it was his turn. "I'm between things," he said.

"Good for you. Sit one out and think about it."

"I'm currently on a ramble."

Ernest chewed at the corner of his mouth. "I'd say we're about the same vintage. What are you, forty-seven or thereabouts?"

"Forty-three." Gibbs offered an abridged version of his run west, leaving out the parts that a man alone in an ice shanty with an ex-con might not care to know. There wasn't much to say.

"Hold on there, friend," Ernest said. He jiggered the rod, sang out, "Fish on the line!" He reeled in smoothly, eventually pulling a perch up through the gray water and smacking it smartly about the head. "Let's put this in the fridge." Ernest opened the door, dropped the fish on the ice. "Cold enough to turn shit blue out there. You were saying."

"A crony of mine used to tell me stories. I figure I had to see this place for myself before it was all said and done. Just to see if he was jerking my chain or not." Considering what had come of Hokanson, some of the stories were no doubt hogwash and prison fiction. He'd even told one that included the motion picture actress Betty Hutton. But he'd said other things, too. Gibbs could get behind the idea of mining gold.

"Ah, the lure of the west," Ernest said. "Not the first man

to be seduced by it and won't be the last. But it's a true thing, the promise of it all. Else they wouldn't say it."

"I hope so," Gibbs said. "You're throwing a rope to a drowning man."

"Just look at you," Ernest said. "A tall stranger riding into town. Like what you used to hear off the radio serials, the shoot-'em-ups. How did it go? 'His skin is sun-dyed brown, the gun in his holster is gray steel and rainbow mother-of-pearl, its handle unmarked.'"

From deep memory Gibbs recalled the rest, joined in, "'People call them both the Six-Shooter.'"

They laughed, Ernest dabbing his eyes with the heel of his palm. "We are such old farts, we don't even smell anymore."

They discussed what the world was coming to. Ernest talked about growing up in these woods. "That river you seen on your way up here. We used to tie one end of a length of rope around a stout tree, the other end around your waist. The spring melt would be spilling down gangbusters and we'd jump in the water like that, snap to the end of the line like a fish. The ride of your life. And *cold*. I swear you could sneeze ice cubes. When we got a bit older we used to take girls out there, have them climb on our backs. I tell you, a girl on your back in a cold river that's yelling watery death in your ears. It was like . . ." He ran a hand through his hair. "Well, like a young girl on your back in the cold water."

"It sounds like a time," Gibbs agreed. He could remember tuning in to the serials with his father, the console about as big as a Stutz Bearcat. He thought again of his brother Miles, the authorities having already phoned him, informing him that Gibbs had jumped parole.

The bell on his tip-up rang like a telephone.

"Heigh ho, friend. Hop to. Fish on the line."

GIBBS FELL ASLEEP from the heat of the shanty, and roused to the ice pack expanding like a crack of a gun. He couldn't at first place where he was, the echo from the depths jarring loose memories of the sharpshooter's rifle sounding in the boggy scrublands outside the wall.

He woke to himself idly sizing up the immediate world of the shanty, eyeing the contents of the ice bob, the surprise of finding amid the crowded shelves what appeared to be a small bear, a primitive terra-cotta handwork of pre-Columbian origin, possibly a tomb figure not worth much. From where he sat he couldn't make it out any better than that. It could have just been an odd-shaped rock. But it got Gibbs wondering anyway, if it was a piece Ernest might have encountered along his trash route, a case of someone not knowing what they had. He wondered, too, what other items of interest the hut might contain. Perhaps Ernest kept a gun for the grizzlies. Even so, Gibbs didn't expect too much fight from the chatterbox. He considered the patchwork of clouds quilting the blue; he himself had the antique sidearm back in the Chrysler.

Ernest crouched over a gas Coleman, a *whooshing* of its

jets. "You got quite the snore, friend, that and the whistling sound from your nose. A bigger commotion than a brass band."

Outside a wind swirled from the empty, wooded hills, shaking the shelter down to its two-by-four blocks, and for a time that's all Gibbs heard, the rushing air. He closed his eyes again, thought of Hokanson's chinooks, the fact that all it took was a favorable wind, the possibility of everything turning in a moment.

He sensed the opportunity for action slipping away and let it, the fading prospect of knocking over Ernest leaving a taste of iron in his mouth, cramping his insides like a vise. He'd heard of cons back at Pine River shitting themselves like babies after losing the nerve and fire for the business, and maybe a bit of that was beginning to happen to him now.

Ernest diced a slab of bacon, cooked it over a low flame, the bacon popping like Chinese firecrackers. He decanted the grease into a jar, added a can of kernel corn to the bacon, a chopped bell pepper and five eggs, then fired another burner, gilled and boned two of the perch and broiled them, using the ice skimmer in lieu of a pan.

"It smells like Thanksgiving in here," Gibbs said, voice thick with sleep, not quite sure he could manage food.

"I wouldn't know about that. The last few years my nose has gone deaf on me. At least you can die saying you had some of Ernest's apache corn."

The two men in the tight confines of the shack—it reminded Gibbs of Pine River.

"Don't be bashful," Ernest said. "A growing boy like you."

Gibbs dug in and it was good, the chow, its heat momentarily jabbing a nerve in a tooth.

"You were looking a little indisposed back there," Ernest said. "Girl trouble, right?"

Gibbs reddened. "I was thinking about my brother," he lied. "Haven't seen him in a long time. His two kids wouldn't know me from Adam."

"Family problems," Ernest said, setting a coffeepot on a burner. "Biggest tragedy of them all. Shakespeare would have been out of business if it weren't for families."

Gibbs stared into the ice holes, like deep-set eyes. "My brother—a scientist. He used to tell me how the littlest drop of blood could tell you all about a person. A lot of things change in life but some don't."

Ernest emptied the grounds directly into the boiling water. "What, like a disease?"

"Maybe," Gibbs said.

Ernest screwed up his face. "I don't know anything about that. Unless it's a cat he was talking about. Nothing you can do with a cat. An established fact of nature." The smell of brewing rose in the shack. "It's a big life, though. Full of surprises. Just look at you."

"Just look at me," Gibbs said.

"One day, you never been ice fishing. The next day, you have."

Ernest retrieved two mugs hanging on hooks and poured

out the coffee. He opened a cabinet on the wall, withdrew a pint. "How about some sweetener? Guaranteed to wash away the blues."

"My drinking days are over," Gibbs said. "If I have a whisky, it makes me feel like a new man. The only problem is, pretty soon the new man starts wanting a whisky, too."

"I hear you. Stuff will kill you." Ernest added a splash to his mug. "Ah me, it'll be my funeral." He helped Gibbs with the tip-up, this time rigging a topwater spool, baiting the lure with mousie grubs, and into the afternoon they fished.

A LIGHT SNOW snicked and whisked against the windows, the day darkening, sun dipping behind the hills, only past four in the afternoon but good as night. Ernest suggested taking a sweat in the sauna he'd built. It was snugged in a swale onshore, had rough-hewn boards, a door that looked like the portal to an elf's house.

It was raw enough to freeze the stuff in Gibbs's nose when they left the fish house. He'd brought only a greasy mac from Jersey and he balled his hands under his armpits. Out on the road, the Chrysler sat collecting flakes.

The building consisted of two rooms. Gibbs ducked into the outer room's soupy dark, a slip of a space with hooks on the wall, a narrow bench, wooden slatwork over a stone foundation. A door opened onto a second chamber and this was larger, a steel tub containing granite stones situated to one side. Underneath this, a woodstove which Ernest mended with splits of piss fir and lodgepole pine. Two tiers of wooden benches were fastened against the wall across from the stove. In the corner of the room, Ernest had sunk a tub into the floor, an overhead shower above the drain, a contraption that stored water which could be heated from the fire for a proper shower.

Gibbs whistled. "You're a busy little booger, aren't you?"

"Idle hands," Ernest said. "One head, a lot of hats."

The two men stripped down in the anteroom. The sauna chamber was hotter than before, smelled of wood. "Engelmann spruce," Ernest said, indicating the benches and walls. Gibbs's glasses misted over and he removed them, the room softening. Ernest poured a dipper of water seasoned with red cedar onto the hot granite stones, which sizzled, a greenish scent rising. "The Indian influence," he explained. "The sweat lodge tradition." He proffered a cigar. "I don't have a peace pipe but I do have these."

The men smoked and dripped.

Even without his glasses, Gibbs noticed Ernest staring at his arm, his biceps, his tattoo, an interlocking design from a Grecian urn, the number thirteen and a half, the handiwork of a con at Pine River who'd adapted an electric razor and length of guitar string for the purpose.

"You put the pin to the skin," Ernest said.

"It seemed like a good idea at the time."

"Twelve jurors, one judge, and one half-assed chance. I've done that, too. The house of pain. My hellcat days. Mostly drunk and disorderlies."

Gibbs said, "I'm basically an antique dealer gone bad.

Once upon a time, I worked the legal end of the trade but that never amounted to much more than pin money."

He explained how he liked old things. Put an old thing in his hand and it spoke to him, told a story, had always been this way. Back as a little kid, his old man had somehow come into a handful of pieces of eight, reales from the Potosí mines in Bolivia, the first mint in the new world. Even before Gibbs could read he sensed the magic in the coins, sat for wordless hours studying them. And later, they held his interest in a way school never did, the rogue accounts of Pizarro in the steeps of the Andes, amazing that so much could be bound in those rough, tarnished circles of silver.

"Counterfeits carry a different sort of story," Gibbs said. "Actually two stories." There was the one that got recounted to customers and then the actual truth of the work's pedigree, each intertwined around the other, snakes coiled on a scepter. The trick had been hawking a piece authentic enough and he'd been cunning in that end of it, ferreting out jewelers on the downside of their careers, individuals with too few scruples and too many bills, who'd not think twice about using their craft to disguise their cast marks on a mold for a phonied-up bronze. But it was the other half of the equation, conjuring a history equally true, that had from time to time tripped him up. Gibbs owned an erratic gift of blarney: it came and went. There was more he could have told, the occasions he'd had to employ his hands rather than his mouth to see a deal through, but he left all that in the shadows.

Ernest said, "Sounds like you put the tits on the monkey."

"The what?"

"You did it up right. I can respect a man who does it up right even if it's a wrong thing he's doing." Ernest rubbed his jawline. "You're a betting man. That's how I read you. A man who relishes a ticklish situation."

"I do have the danger gene," Gibbs agreed. He pulled on the cigar, exhaled smoke out the side of his mouth, waving a hand to disperse it. "There was this dealer once," he said. "A hundred years ago. In London." He couldn't recall the fellow's name, only the boys he used to send into the Thames: mudboys, they were called—Billy and Charley. The story went that these mudboys would emerge from the river with artifacts of ungodly value. Coats of arms in openwork medallions. Oil lamps from the Roman era. Bronze Medusas.

"Here's the thing," Gibbs said.

Ernest nodded. "There's always a thing."

"The dealer, he made a tidy fortune on the stock and word spread and then, wouldn't you know, somebody was always finding something on a piece that didn't quite make sense, shouldn't have been there. Turns out the whole lot is a trove of fantasy pieces. The mudboys just made for a more convincing story."

The fire ticked in the stove.

"It's crazy," Gibbs continued. "The pieces the mudboys excavated—there's actually a market for them now. Called Billy-and-Charleys."

"You're shitting me."

"I shit you not."

Ernest ladled water onto the fire and the granite stones spat. "I suppose if enough time goes by, anything can happen. You should live so long. We both should."

Outside it was dark and only that. The lantern cast a sallow shine, their indistinct shadows on the walls.

"I would like to think that part of my life is over," Gibbs said.

Their sweat hitting the benches: like a light rain.

Ernest stuck the cigar in the corner of his mouth. "You were thinking of taking me down," he said evenly. "Before. Back in the shanty. In the afternoon."

Gibbs took the cigar from his mouth, placed it on the bench, felt the other man's eyes on him. He inspected the back of his hands, his face flushing from shame, from the dry fire of the sauna. "I didn't, though," he said. "That should be worth something."

"It wouldn't have been sporting. Me teaching you fishing."

"No, it wouldn't have been." It was somehow worse without his glasses. He wiped the lenses on the end of a towel, fit them on, found Ernest watching him more than carefully, and removed his glasses again. "I guess I should go," he said.

The men dressed in the anteroom, Ernest like a fever blister in his red union suit. "But you're right, pal," he said. "You didn't do it. You didn't roll me. Far be it from me to hold you accountable for a thing you didn't do."

It was cooler in the dressing room. Gibbs leaned against the back wall, could feel the cold from the outside but remained hot from the sauna.

"The Finnish people," Ernest said, "typically roll in the snow after taking in a sauna." He smiled. "I could always use another hand for my trash hauling business. A good back. You just might happen on some diamonds in the rough. I could tell you stories."

"You shame me, Ernest."

"You're not such a bad man."

"Sometimes I don't know."

"Take it from Ernest then."

"There's this place I still want to get to," Gibbs said.

Out on the ice, steam ascended from their heads.

"That would be you up there," Ernest said, pointing to the Chrysler. A moon had lifted above the timbered hill, its light thrown across the lake and snowy ground. There were more stars than Gibbs had ever seen, the night stippled with them.

"I jacked the car," Gibbs said. "Back in Jersey."

Ernest blinked. "You didn't kill anybody."

"No."

"There you go. I'd say you're rehabilitated."

They laughed, the sound of it carrying across the frozen water. It was frosty, the effects of the sauna wearing off.

"Fish on the line," Gibbs said.

"Right-o," Ernest said and they shook on it.

On his way back to the Chrysler, Gibbs glanced over his shoulder, Ernest in his union suit, a reddish blob against a white field of hills but nothing that might look like a mine.

"Hey!" he yelled. "What is this place?"

"Here?" Ernest puffed on the last of his cigar. "This is officially nowhere."

Gibbs threw a wave, like a man erasing a blackboard, then continued toward the snow-clad vehicle.

GIBBS FELT SO CHEAP after the ice fishing he could have been bought all day long for a penny. He'd hoped that he'd put distance between him and his old self, that it was left back there, along the road, like so much other trash, but his afternoon with Ernest had chased more than a little of that optimism.

He thought about Jolie. He'd not suffered a minute's remorse before then for making off with her mad money, sailing out of her life, not so much as a note. These were people— Jolie and Ernest, too—who'd cared for him, taken him in, and look how he'd acted.

He'd known her from the bars where he'd once bent elbows though it was only after he'd stopped drinking, after his last stint at the facilities, that they hooked up. A little thing: blond hair from one bottle, tan skin from another, a tattoo along the bikini line of her hip that read DO YOU WANT TO DANCE. It'd been hunky-dory for a while, his early days out from the wall, Jolie returning home from the graveyard shift at the bakery, a flecking of maple frosting still on her. Outside, the sun hoisted over a gray ocean and Gibbs licked her like a postage stamp from stem to stern.

His thieving past had excited her. She also liked things on the rough side and for a while he liked that, too. "Isn't that how they did it in the pokey?" she'd tease him. "Isn't this how it was done?" It was new and seemed like kicks but over time it'd only reminded him of all he cared to forget, didn't feel like any love he'd ever hoped for, only one more wall in his life, one more thing he didn't have use for any longer.

NOW, GIBBS RECALLED the thrumming animal rush of his run. Aside from the two wrongs—stealing the car and Jolie's money—he'd not done anything else wrong since. His thoughts were a different story. But as Ernest had said, you couldn't hold a man accountable for ideas that never grew legs.

Gibbs decided he still needed to road dog until he happened on the right situation. Luck couldn't avoid him all his life.

He fired the Chrysler, drove to the south and west, and Montana remade itself, the bunched, scoliotic spines of mountains spreading out until they were bookends on the sides of far valleys, the habitations in the lee of distant hills. Rails traced the outline of the road for a while and then not.

He motored the Bitterroots, then mining country, the towns that got fat a century ago, the avenue buildings constructed of brick, made to last. He lodged in seedier accommodations, a nod to economy, fearing the day when his roll would unpeel to zip. He'd not counted the money—it felt like bad luck to do so—but he'd steadily nibbled away at it like a holiday roast, didn't know what would happen after he reached the bottom of his pocket.

At the edge of town the high plains met the main, the mountains on the western horizon hooded in snow, not unlike the sugar-dusted crullers Jolie sometimes brought back from the bakery. Gibbs studied them, as if the place he still hankered to get to might blow in from there. The locals hurried about their business, pickups loaded down, townspeople walking the streets bent with purpose, all of it a world unconnected to his own. It was only the wind that blew in from the mountains and if it spoke of anything, it was winter.

AND THEN ONE MORNING Gibbs woke to a crown going off in his head. His teeth were never any good and ham-fisted prison dentistry hadn't improved matters any. The nerve howled like an alarm, like it was jerked on a string all the way back to Jersey, and he took it as an omen.

He made for the western mountains, a blustery day, a sky like bleach. It must have snowed up high during the night, certainly chill enough, the mountains now entirely covered in an enamel of white, and he drove toward them for the better part of the day. Nearing the foothills, the road began to climb and, off to one side, a weather-beaten mining flume girded the shoulder of hill.

A sign along the road indicated the Continental Divide ahead, the falling snow not much at first, spokes of bluestem grass still sticking out of the spotty carpet that had accumulated. And then more, the air a white screen. A few more sheer miles and he was in the chowdery thick of it, the blizzard splitting the season like a frozen maul.

Late afternoon and then twilight. Both Gibbs and the Chrysler running feverish, the infection in his sick tooth, the car missing every now and then. The road rose in a ladder of switchbacks, only the mess of horizontal weather, everything else erased in the swirl. Gibbs stood on the pedal, the engine hammering more than a tinker's workshop.

It was only when he crested the pass that he saw them— the horses. They ran ahead, somewhere beyond the throw of the headlights. A snow mirage, he thought at first. Then he caught them again in the television static of the storm: a kick of hooves, flickers of rumps big as ship sterns. Gibbs was on the western side of the divide now, where the rivers flowed to the opposite end of the continent, to a different ocean, and it seemed possible he could be chasing a gang of wild mustangs through a stone-blind snow.

The roadway tipped down and momentum carried the Chrysler forward. The scratch of wipers on the windshield. He strained for another glimpse but they were gone, his glasses not of much help anyway, two prescriptions behind what they ought to be. After a few miles of descent, the living world came into view: tree line, aspens plumb as flagpoles, then clumps of red willow, and then an occasional split-wood fence amid the snowfields.

Gibbs more sledded than drove. As he rounded a bend, his beams locked on a lone horse in a paddock, not one of the stampede, but a roan so emaciated it could have been a stick-figure drawing. He stopped. No house or barn, only the horse in white up to its knees, its tumble-down pen. The two regarded each other for several minutes. Gibbs debated whether to set it free. It could get hit by a car, not any kinder fate than freezing to death right here.

The Chrysler sounded like it was eating itself. He assumed the glinting lights were a constellation of stars, so far away. But they couldn't have been: Gibbs was above them. Flakes fell out of the coarse night and he stared at the winking bracelet, at the lights in the valley below.

THE CHRYSLER SEIZED UP for good in the flats at the outskirts of town and he plodded the remaining distance on foot. A sign read LADLE and beyond that another, of homemade variety, GO AWAY.

Wind scared up snow ghosts, the town like something out of a Lionel train set, a run of buildings of board-and-batten construction on either side of the street. A string of lights shook, the yaw of a gooseneck lamp on its mooring.

He pitched through the drifts like a man on stilts. It was only when circling back to the other side of the street that he spotted the dry goods store in an alley, the faint luster of a burning bulb behind a fogged shop window. The door opened onto a dusty room, two runs of deep wooden shelves for aisles, burlap sacks of rice and grain along the wall as well as tack and feed. A graying woman behind the counter, a beatific face that said she might have been expecting him for ages. A fire cracked in a potbellied stove. Gibbs tracked snow across a floor scuffed the color of tobacco.

"The first storm of the season," she said, as if the answer to a question he might have asked and maybe he had.

The shelves contained a motley assortment—tins of kippers and jellies, sourdough mix. He'd not thought of his tooth for a long time and now he did, its spiking twinge. He must have looked ridiculous, snow capping his hatless head, epaulets of it across the shoulders of his mac. Gibbs told her of the white-knuckle ride down the divide. The last miles of the descent the heater had surrendered, then the wipers and power steering, and he'd the sensation of going down in a plane, searching for the best place to ditch.

As he talked, he noticed, high on a shelf above the woman's head, a bronze known as Christ of the Tender Mercy if he could trust his eyes, a highly prized collectible. He himself had traded in a counterfeit of the piece, coating it with varnish to fake the patina of age.

"Is there a dentist in town?" he asked.

"Brownie might be of help with the car," the woman told him.

"Brownie," Gibbs said, as if a name he should know.

"He's the only one left in Ladle who can figure cars. Brownie would be the one." She glanced at her watch. "He's probably at the Silver Cloud. The roadhouse." She gave directions, through the alley, behind the shuttered-up buildings on the main. "You'll see the red from the beer signs."

The lights dimmed, a brownout, then the electricity catching, the click and whir of refrigeration starting up.

"Thank you," Gibbs said, feet clomping toward the door, which opened with a shiver of bells. He turned, squinted up at the high shelf. "You know, that's a Christ of the Tender Mercy," he ventured before leaving, gesturing up at the bronze. He'd have liked to take the step-ladder over, to make sure.

The woman smiled, eyes nearly closed. "Yes," she said. "Yes, He certainly is."

ON THE OUTSIDE the Silver Cloud appeared normal enough. The inside, however, was fashioned after a maritime passenger ship, the tavern in the front done up like a quarterdeck: a railing on one side of the room, an oceanscape painted beyond it; a row of portholes that looked out onto the snowy world; in one corner, a lifeboat slung to davits, a web of standing rigging held fast in lanyards and deadeyes; over by the billiards table, a ventilator cowl, upthrust like a brass mushroom.

It was in the back room where he found Brownie, playing poker with three others. Gibbs stood in the doorway and watched, the quarters modeled after a stateroom, walls bloodied burgundy, streaky with water stains, a fire blazing away in the hearth. Overhead, a pendant lamp of flash copper, the plaster ceiling in a couple of areas eaten away, the tin roof above as well, and snow fell through the gap, shaking out like rock salt down into cookpots.

Much later it would all seem to Gibbs as though the four could have been playing cards for days, or quite possibly forever, this strange, beached ship in the high mountains, the sea of snow.

The storm raged like an animal that wanted in.

"I'm looking for someone called Brownie," Gibbs said.

A sprite of a man, a beard like deer moss on his chin, said, "That would be me."

"I got some business with a car," Gibbs said.

"Maybe you care to join us. Our little kitchen table game."

The dying nerve in Gibbs's mouth banged away, a nail being driven into his head. There was no place else for him to go and he could do with extra funds, not down to scared money but close. Gibbs listened to the wolf wind, as if that could decide it for him, but to his eyes, there was only trouble inhabiting this room. He told them thanks but no thanks, told this Brownie he'd wait up front for him.

At the bar in the quarterdeck tavern, he allowed the lady bartender to pour a club soda. In the corner by the lifeboat, a jukebox all lit up like the county fair. A small crowd was in from the storm, their talk largely speculation regarding its severity and duration, a few having snowshoed, their gear leaning by the door, cakes of snow melting on the deck flooring, mostly men, canvas coats still on their backs.

Gibbs sat amidst the gabble of conversation, a mongrel aroma of smoke, sweat, booze. From behind someone said, "It'll be a bumpy ride." And then from another end of the room, as if answering it, "You got the soul of a fat woman."

A few stools down the line, a couple of smart alecks getting pleasantly stinko, arm-wrestling for drinks and cigars. Gibbs considered his options and there wasn't much to consider. He thought about the poker, the open seat at the table tempting him like an open bottle.

He was relieved when somebody took the bar stool next to him. "It's freezing," he found himself saying.

"A good blow," the fellow agreed and told Gibbs it was nothing like Alaska where he once worked, running gravel for the oil concerns. Gibbs had heard about that, the money to be made, and was glad to think about something else besides the pull of the other room.

They carried on. Gibbs recounted seeing some fool in a bear costume waving customers to a diner in Battle Lake, Minnesota, during his run out, and they laughed about how crazy the world was. They reached the bottom of their glasses at roughly the same time and Gibbs offered the next round.

"Oh no, you don't," the fellow said. "You don't pull coin in my town."

"Okay, club soda then," Gibbs said.

"The wagon?"

"Afraid so."

"Sobering," the other man said. "Sounds an awful lot like 'so boring,' doesn't it?"

After a while, he left Gibbs at the bar alone. All the forward motion of the run collected within, like a hunger, nowhere else to go. He thought of Hokanson, the lights-out stories, one feeding to another until what bobbed to the surface was the one that concerned Betty Hutton.

It'd occurred during the war. She'd been on some sort of tour to spur the boys in the ore drifts, give them cheer for their end of the effort. If Gibbs remembered it right, there'd been a storm then, too. Betty was only supposed to visit an afternoon, a few hours, but wound up weathered in for days, this the first blush of her fame and she glowed brighter than anything the mines would ever excavate, like magic, the days snowbound in town, the world lost behind the storm, only Betty and a hundred lucky souls.

There was the usual that one might expect, Betty giving her heart—and perhaps a bit more—to some of the local men. But what remained glued in Gibbs's mind was not that. "She promised she'd be back," Hokanson had rasped. The presence of Betty in the town had lent the place a quality it'd not owned before, given it hope, made it somehow bigger. On her last night, she'd stood atop the bar in the saloon, blond hair shiny as bullion, and belted "Let's Not Talk About Love," her hit song of the time, stopping shy of the big ending in the final verse, telling the gathered people she'd finish it properly for them upon her return. "One more reason so you don't forget me," Betty had said, winking at the lot of them.

According to Hokanson, though, she never visited again, only word of her motion pictures making their way to town from time to time, her snapshot in magazines. "She said she'd be back," Hokanson had said. "People are still waiting for her."

Listening to the story in the narrow raft of his bunk, Gibbs had thought maybe Betty Hutton was dead and that explained it but he said nothing. Later, after Hokanson had flown, he ran across a story on her in a *Life* magazine, in the prison library, and she was indeed alive. It'd been a tough life, more disappointment than joy perhaps, a bad marriage and a stalled career, a brief comeback in the fifties, a stage show where she fired six-shooters and sang a medley of her movie hits, but it didn't last. And Gibbs could understand why she might have broken the promise. And it seemed sad to him, the saddest thing, what age and life could do, that Betty Hutton wasn't even Betty Hutton anymore and if she had returned, would anybody have recognized her even so?

Gibbs surveyed the tavern now. He could not recall the name of that town but it struck him that this could have been it, the beaten, lined expressions on the folks around him, faces that said that they might be waiting out more than just the end of a blizzard. He searched the walls, the flotsam of nautical gewgaws—standing blocks and capstans and running lights— but no evidence of Betty, no autographed, fading glamour shot, and Hokanson had never mentioned a bar that looked like a ship anyway.

IT SNOWED AND SNOWED.

Hours later the game broke for refreshment, the four men walking up from the back room. There was a fat man, perhaps the fattest Gibbs had ever seen, and he took a seat in a corner booth. The two players besides Brownie were mouthy types, one with an ill-advised mustache like a push broom. The other, older and a little worse for wear, limped like he had a sack of nails in his shoe, a *pop-siss* that Gibbs realized must be a prosthetic leg. Both were done up in checked cowboy shirts and looked like idiots.

From up at the bar, Gibbs observed the four with interest. He did not need to be in the game to understand what was going down, had sat in on enough poker to know the story. The idiots were obviously a couple of rammer-jammers who'd blown into town before him, had the good fortune of catching the heater of their life, every card falling their way; they were unbeatable. Perhaps, too, they were riding more than a hot streak—from their antics at the pool table, Gibbs would have guessed cheap trucker speed.

He could not get a read on the fat man in the corner or Brownie, who'd settled into a nearby booth. Gibbs walked over, sat down without invitation, told the little man about the trials of the Chrysler.

"That's a real unfortunate story," Brownie said when Gibbs was done, his eyes red-rimmed and small as scattershot.

Gibbs did not want to be there. The game would turn, as it always did, and then there'd be hell to pay one way or the other and he wanted to be miles distant by then.

Brownie said, "There's nothing I can do, seeing as I'm conducting business back there."

The lady bartender asked for food orders and Brownie simply nodded at her and Gibbs ordered a dish called red flannel hash because it sounded like something he could choke down without much chewing. He'd not eaten since his tooth went off that morning, since his flyer into the mountains.

The two men watched the flakes spill down on the other side of the porthole, the evening lost in tatters of white.

"What is this place anyway?" Gibbs asked.

"What is this place," Brownie said and then told him and Gibbs leaned forward to hear it, hoping maybe it'd be the Betty Hutton story but it wasn't.

"Believe it or not this used to be somewhere," Brownie said. "A company town. Mining. They own everything here down to the nails. This establishment included."

Gibbs tried to imagine it but couldn't. All he could see was a forgotten nest in the mountains.

"They're closing us down," Brownie said. "Once was thirteen thousand of us, during the boom years. Now hardly a handful left. An end to a life." He smoothed the tablecloth. "Welcome to Ladle, mister."

Gibbs thought the little man might cry. A shelf of snow slid off the tin roof: a deep rumble, like continents shifting.

"It's not been a good year," Brownie continued. On top of it all, his dog up and died on him, a Heinz 57. He pulled a photo from his shirt pocket. "One of those supermarket dogs, the kind they have out front. So gentle it wouldn't bite its own fleas." He'd buried and dug it up five times, not wanting to believe, hoping it was just a seizure or something. "Friends— they come and go. But a dog is a dog."

The talk of Brownie's mutt reminded Gibbs of the spectral run of the horses he'd seen after topping the divide and they galloped through him again. "I saw some horses," he said. "On my way in before the car died. Wild horses."

Brownie considered him balefully. "I don't know anything about that."

From over at the billiards table, the ruckus of the two jokers in checked cowboy shirts, the rammer-jammers. Brownie and Gibbs glanced over, Brownie lifting an eyebrow.

"You could still buy into the game," he said and told Gibbs that they'd all agreed to play until the snow stopped.

The bartender conveyed a tray of food down to the fat man in the corner, so many platters it could have fed a small battalion.

"You want to know about Tap," Brownie said. Gibbs did not care to know, only wanted out. Brownie told him anyway, about a terrible mining accident years ago concerning a fraternal twin brother, this Ladle seeming to be somewhere peopled with more desolate stories than actual souls, as far away from that place he'd longed to reach as the moon.

Across the table, the little man, flinty as a prospector or at least what Gibbs thought a prospector should look like. He suspected he'd encountered Brownie's sort before, that they might not have been very different men at all, his wrist bearing a spidery tattoo with all the earmarks of prison scratch: old, but like it might have been still bleeding.

Gibbs held up both hands, as if in surrender. "I'm doing my best here to be a standup citizen. The hardest thing in the world sometimes."

Their food arrived, the red flannel hash the consistency of prison chow, a brick-colored slurry, but tasted better, Brownie's fare a slab of unspecified meat, orange as neon. Gibbs stared at it.

"What," Brownie said, "you never seen elk before?"

"What is that," Gibbs said, "some kind of deer?"

They busied themselves with their food. The men, Gibbs knew, would return soon to the card table, the stateroom drawing on him like a tide or gravity. He sucked on his fouled tooth, the pain offering something else to focus on. From out of the blue, he remembered that Claire woman from Glacier, her kid Elliot, his first day in Montana, the trust she'd extended. It felt like long ago to Gibbs, like an antique he still wished he owned.

AFTER HOKANSON HAD ESCAPED Pine River the entire cell-block was put under lockdown, Gibbs thrown into the hole once the battery of interrogation had run its course. He'd nothing to tell, could have told any of a hundred stories, the scrape of Hokanson's voice covering the scrape of his jerry-built file across the heating vent above his upper bunk, the one-word note left under his pillow, *Smile.*

He thought of this after the four cardplayers resumed the game. It was just possible that the Chrysler was hale again, that all it needed was to cool down after the ordeal of climbing the divide. Cars had their own agenda and Gibbs never fully understood them.

The world on the other side of the door was unlike any he'd ever witnessed, the midnight sky flinging lightning now in addition to snow, forks walking the shoulders of mountain, illuminating the peaks. With the drifts piled waist-high and higher, it was more like swimming than striding, the cold cracking the left lens of his glasses, numbing his extremities into clubs, boring a hole though the inflamed nerve in his jaw, up into his head.

Somewhere, a bell ringing or maybe just the wind.

It was a fight to keep on, and what Gibbs thought about to hold off the cold were all the various brawls he'd been in. He would have liked to say he didn't like hitting people although he had certainly done that. A fight had sent him to Pine River, the result of a ruinous transaction of no-good works of figurative jewelry he couldn't move, Gibbs resorting to strong-arm methods to set things aright. The subsequent fact of fraud, a broken nose and a shattered cheekbone had made it aggravated circumstances and, as a matter of course, he'd graduated to a new level of convict. It was not the first time he'd relied on such tactics in a business dealing. Sometimes it hadn't even been called for but he'd done so anyway because he felt it'd been expected from a person like him. And, of course, the scuf-fles in his drinking days. Whisky used to turn him into some-one else. He remembered one time breaking a bottle over a man's head for the crime of telling a joke wrong.

Every freezing step, another fracas. Gibbs had walked clear of Ladle, the buildings on the main appearing over his shoulder in a snap of lightning. Back as kids, he'd beat on Miles for the sport of it, because he could. And Gibbs gasped at it all, the icy intake of air, wind tearing a hole in his face.

The Chrysler was nowhere to be seen. Gibbs spun a tight circle in the drifts. The signs had disappeared, the one that read LADLE and the other, GO AWAY. It occurred to Gibbs then that perhaps he was on top of the car, that it'd snowed that much, and he spotted the last of the whip antenna sticking out of the white like a hank of unruly hair, dug down with bare hands, located the back door, clearing around so it could swing open, the dome light still working but nothing else, like a coffin inside.

Gibbs sat in the backseat. He could remain, allow the bliz-zard to pile up over the car, a prison of snow. He tried to keep his teeth from chattering but it was no good, a feeling like someone twirling his failing crown by the root. Hokanson's chinook winds blew into mind except the process seemed to be working the other way, fall turning to winter in a matter of hours, this the other side of the coin, he realized, like some law of physics, that if a life could be redeemed in a moment, it could go south just as fast.

Next to him on the seat, between his satchel of effects and the sack of counterfeit works, the familiar wooden handle of the sidearm which looked like two handles, the refraction of his cracked lens. He pulled it out, took it in hand, examined the piece like an answer to a question he'd not yet asked, the bluing on the barrel gone to pitch, the curly filigrees above the trigger. The old man used to finger it when they listened to the serials, a few splashes in his glass to chase the hours of operating the elevator, the up and down and never going anywhere, all of it held at bay for a time by whisky and myth.

Gibbs mulled it over but there was really no other option. He gathered up the phonied works, tucked the gun into his waistband of his slacks, left the satchel where it was, and stepped out into the riot of flakes. He retraced his footprints, the occasional glint of lightning, boom of thunder. Along the way, he peered in the window of the dry goods store he'd stopped in earlier. No lights burning, no bronze of Christ of the Tender Mercy on the high shelf, only dust cloths shrouding every surface, like it'd been closed for years.

HE SAT DOWN TO a different game from before. There was the spiral of snow threading through the gap of roof and the four other men at the table, the bench to the upright piano in the corner broken up for firewood.

But it was a different game. Nobody'd bothered to tell the pair in the checked cowboy shirts that the heater they'd caught like a rocket was fast crashing back to earth. They tried to bull the action even so, their chips rapidly traveling across the table, some to Gibbs but mostly the other two, the fat man, Tap, wagering in the softest voice, oily as tallow, Gibbs recalling the mining-accident story that Brownie'd told about the twin brother, a loss that Tap appeared to be grieving yet.

They played cards—Omaha and lowball, stud and draw. Sometime in the little hours, the lights blacked out. "The weight of snow on the lines," Brownie said, lighting a lantern.

The hours swam as in Gibbs's drinking days of old. When they broke for food one last time, he visited the bathroom instead, lit a match to see himself in the mirror, retracted his cheek to inspect the angry red of his gumline, a haggard face staring back at him from the dark, worn as a shoe. He was up in the game but couldn't count on it lasting, and the thought of what lay ahead only made him tired. He retreated to the stall toilet, sat on the can, propped his feet on the metal partition and dozed.

He woke to the two clowns banging lines on the sink counter, hatching a plan for what would come next.

"We should sack these boys," the one with the push-broom mustache said. "I tell you, they'll never know what hit."

"I don't know," the peg leg answered.

"Then why don't we just hand over all the rest of our money?" Mustache had a voice like a needle.

"What about the stranger?" Peg Leg wanted to know.

"The lummox?" Mustache said. "The lummox concerns me."

Gibbs didn't move for a long time after the boys quit the rest room, sat there, felt his legs going back toward the room even before they were under him, as inevitable as riverflow.

ALL THE CRAZY GAMES walked out of the deck once the poker reconvened, the pot limits thrown through the holes in the ceiling, what Brownie and the fat man had been waiting for all along, the rash play of losing men wanting to once more own the universe. The cards circled the table—hands of southern cross, wild widow, butcher boy—the lantern's modest cast on the bloody walls, like the inside of Gibbs's mouth, like the deer meat that Brownie had supped on earlier, elk he'd called it. The two rammer-jammers began fortifying their toot and resolve with grain alcohol, operating on full tilt. Gibbs played like a leather ass, mucking his cards more often than not, no longer concerned with the outcome of hands, waiting only for the pair to do something stupid, then he would do something, the gun barrel of the six-shooter sticking the shank of his hip like an insistent idea.

It didn't happen like that. The burn Mustache had been riding finally consumed him, knocking him out flat, stranding his pal in the game. And then dawn. They didn't notice at first, the storm having blown out, leaving in its wake a white-swept expanse, a sapphire sky through the ceiling, the last flakes sifting in like talc.

It was Gibbs's deal and he heard again Hokanson, the scratchy voice: "She'd said she'd be back." And it would all come down to this, the two words he'd utter next. "Betty

Hutton," Gibbs said. "Some of you might know Kankakee. Betty Hutton is fives and nines wild." They would play the final hand blind, the cards dealt facedown, unseen by the players, a contest of chicken to determine who'd be standing last, Gibbs tired and desperate enough to resign his fate to the disposition of kings and queens.

They wagered after each card, raised in giant steps, beyond reason, until everything was heaped in the middle, four men with nothing else to lose.

Seventh Street, the final card. The fat man pulled a creased deed from a pocket, let it flutter in, the family claim he told them. Brownie tossed in the key to his Willys jeep. Peg Leg scoured himself so thoroughly it seemed he might even unhitch his prosthetic leg and offer that, too. He ransacked Mustache's pockets instead, once his own were down to lint, went as far as disengaging the massive rodeo belt buckle from his slumped confederate, unlooping it, dropping belt and buckle into the pile like an exotic three-foot snake wearing a gold helmet.

Gibbs unpeeled the last of Jolie's mad money, emptied his sack of fantasy works, the gaudy carnelians and jades. He knew from the radio serials what a fellow was supposed to do in such a circumstance and reached in his mouth, pulled the offending crown until it broke loose, a jolt as clarifying and sharp as a white flame.

A small lifetime—his years in rooms overcrowded with men. From outside, chiming voices, kids cavorting in the morning's untracked drifts. He thought of Miles, not the scientist, but them as boys, riding bikes like a couple of cowboys roving the range, a cocked hand all that was needed to convey a gun. And even with his rotten glasses, Gibbs saw it clearer then, what he'd been driving at all this time, since jacking the car and before, not a place, only a feeling, the understanding of what his body could do and had done, the difference of what ran in his blood and resided in his heart. It was an awful truth, just how much his arms had kept the world at a distance, a lonelier confinement than any prison he'd ever know. And for the briefest moment, the wild horses blew through him again, more like a scavenging wind than the roll of hooves this time, then the hopelessness of the immediate situation returning.

He smiled, a new space among the composition of his teeth, the eyes of the others traveling on a wire between the bloody stub of porcelain and gold on the green felt and Gibbs, each of them with a different variation of the same look, like they might have drunk milk that had turned bad.

It would be so easy. If it came to it, he figured he could squeeze off two shots and maybe that would be enough, the sidearm just as liable to blow up in his face as shoot true, which might've been okay, too.

LATER THAT MORNING, Gibbs thought maybe Brownie was trying to welsh on the jeep, the little man bent on showing him the town after that last hand was on the books. He was glad to see the place anyway, all that he'd missed under the cover of dark and weather, the evening before. A morning of sunshine, jeweled glimmer of snow, a sky the color of a pretty girl's eyes.

It was situated in the bottom corner of a canyon, Ladle and the mine. The Silver Cloud was located where the sheer walls met, behind the run of main. With the crust of white, the squared angles of rock, the land reminded Gibbs of an icebox.

Brownie showed him the tailing carts rusting on narrow-gauge tracks, piles of waste rock and slag from the operation. They ducked through the adit and walked a distance into the drift, the sides closing in on Gibbs, and inside the mine he thought not of Hokanson's pie-in-the-sky stories but of Tap, the accident with his twin, that there were worse things that could be visited on a pair of brothers.

Gibbs was unprepared for what he found at Brownie's house. It was a string of structures actually, the old assay office, pay and samples, boiler shop and hoist house cabins, the tin roofs rusted to a fine brown stubble, wood beams silvery with age, Brownie evidently an unofficial caretaker for the dead mine. The buildings contained a staggering collection of antiques—mica windows, walls of painted oilcloth, sinks adapted from the lacquered wood of whisky barrels, like a seashell clasped to his ear, the life Gibbs could hear breathing out. A wall calendar said the right month but wrong year. The newspaper stuffing the stove in one of the cabins dated 1941. In one of the buildings, toys of First World War vintage, in another a lunch bucket left on a counter from forty years before.

He'd the sense of strolling through a museum, a place

frozen in storage, something even more of a miracle than that last hand of Betty Hutton. A hardbound copy of Zane Grey's *Twin Sombreros* sat on a shelf and Gibbs again remembered listening to the shoot-'em-ups on the radio with his old man and it came to him, thumbing the yellowed pages, that perhaps Miles somehow had it wrong, that maybe blood wasn't quite as fixed as he'd said, that what ran in them stepped back through their father, back to the oldest living things, that there was still room for possibility, enough to have produced the both of them.

"I try to keep it how it was," Brownie said.

Gibbs nodded. He stopped cataloging the items when he reached a turn-of-the-century Marvel cookstove, bygone kitchen utensils hanging from the close rafters, stopped guessing the value and just took it in, the buildings ticking like a heart, a time when the outside world had beat a path to Ladle, when it had been a place; Brownie's life, too, his untold days of preserving a thing nobody had use for anymore.

It was real and Gibbs had no words for what he saw. He would be among the last to hear what the town had to say for itself. And he toured the cabins, studied their contents like something he needed to memorize, to fix in mind.

He stood on Brownie's covered porch before taking claim on the Willys and shoving off. From the incline of hill, the town spread out below, the high sides of rockwall, the mountains behind everything, like gears of a terrible machine. The air had a nip to it, but not so bad. A gauzy sickle moon had attached itself in the low blue.

"I thought you might have been a mechanic with the cards," Brownie said. "I watched you deal, though, and it wasn't that. All the fives and nines. Just lucky."

Gibbs leaned over the railing. In the front yard, the snow-capped shape of a '55 De Soto which Brownie told him he'd stopped driving ever since the Arabs monkeyed with the gas prices.

"Lucky," Gibbs said. "I wouldn't have said so." He thought about the word, how it matched up with his life, trying it on like some new hat. "Maybe," he said.

Brownie squinted. "The gems and curios you threw in. They real?"

"Does it matter?" Gibbs said. He considered the avalanche chutes on the slopes ascending back in the direction of the divide. He had gotten someplace, only part of the way to where he had to go, and the remaining distance—he couldn't guess how long that might take. "I suppose it does matter," he said.

From somewhere in the valley, the sound of a radio, a big band tune from the forties, the bell-like tones of a songbird carrying like a breeze, filling up the canyon. The western end of the rockface seemed close enough for Gibbs to reach out and touch, like touching the other side of the earth.

"What are you going to do?" Gibbs asked. "This place."

"We're running out of time," Brownie said. "There's hardly any left."

Gibbs watched the little man, noticed that part of one ear was chewed off, the hangy-down of his lobe, and the idea occurred to him that perhaps Brownie might be dying. "So what happens after?"

"There's talk of a theme park. Tearing all this down to erect a ghost town theme park," Brownie said.

Gibbs shook his head. "The world is a broke-dick operation." He reached into a pocket, found the slip of paper, pulled out the mining claim. "You can give this back to that Tap fella," he said. "I have no use for blood money. I myself have a brother."

Brownie smiled more hard-won than happy. "The clutch will stick on you but you won't be unsatisfied."

They looked at the boxed landscape of snow, rock, sky. Gibbs thought of the buried Chrysler, how next spring when the white receded it'd reveal itself again, one door open, a hulk of metal, and the rest, mystery.

"I expect you'll be going though you don't have to," Brownie told him.

"Oh, I might come back," Gibbs said.

Brownie kicked a mantle of snow from the porch. "Okay, but I won't hold you to it."

LATE AFTERNOON. Gibbs drove west, following a cleft in the canyon, like a roofless tunnel through the mountains. The Willys ran with a constant shout, a body square as a flivver, its backseat containing the contents of the last round of poker: a sack with more money than he might have ever held and the various other spoils.

He climbed in altitude and the landscape unfolded ahead, a dashing stream on one side, rapids white as shaving soap. He had enough scratch to pay Jolie back and still live fat, though he probably wouldn't. He thought about calling his brother, Miles, another thing he'd not do.

On the approaching slope, tree line, the dense network of aspens frosted in new snow, the hills lit in the alpenglow of impending twilight. It was then that he saw them again, the animals. They indeed had the hindquarters of horses but the forequarters were something else entirely. They looked like deer on steroids, that big and chesty. They ran in a clattering herd ahead of him and he followed, goosing the accelerator, attempting to close the distance.

And then the word came to him. "Elk," Gibbs said and laughed, the teeth and gumline around the space in his mouth, where his crown was once, twanging like a guitar string. *Elk,* like the first word of a new language he was only now beginning to learn.

IN THE
SNOW FOREST

Autumn: already the sad loss of autumn.

That fall the Trinities were empty of men, Darby the only one left. The only one who didn't sign on with the logging teams when a private timber concern came through back in August, an outfit operating north out of Cecilville, high and far in the granite hills, the rare opportunity to fell the big sticks till the first snows. He'd had an injury, his shoulder, and were it not for that, the insurance money still flowing to him because of it, Darby would have assuredly been with the rest, making the sawdust fly.

It was a last hurrah and who knew when the next such opportunity would come along. Ever since the door to the woods got shut and the public lands forever closed to logging, the crew looked to a man as if they'd woken up late only to find they'd slept through the best part of a movie. And now here they were, knocking the rust off their saws after all these years, leaving Darby behind with the women and children.

There was one woman and her name was Harper and on Tuesdays Darby lunched with her at the Yellow Jacket, the only eating establishment in forty miles. All Harper had was an afternoon, one day a week, the hours a nurse from county public health made the long drive under the trees to check on her kid. Darby didn't know what exactly was wrong, only that it was terrible, an obscure bone malady, and worse.

The crew had put him up to it, at the fare-thee-well at the Timbers the night before they shoved off, more than one of that lot telling him to look after her. Darby and Harper had never been what might be called friends, him only one of the hurly-burly of desperate men who orbited her on their nights out. She'd fallen in with his crowd the way these things happen, after Adcock quit her and the Trinities for good. "I could use a drink of a certain description," she'd tease the crew slyly. And then, once the initial rounds were slammed down, "Boys, I'm about two shots shy of wonderful."

They lunched on egg sandwiches and curly fries, watched the fixed-wing planes etch sky above the bowl of mountains, the lazy approach over the lake, its surface cupping from prop wash, and then touch down at the midget flyway a stone's throw away. From behind the swinging doors, the clatter of Lynette in the scullery, the air heavy with salt and fried cooking.

It was only one day a week, devoid of romance, unlike anything Darby had known before. The things Harper told him—he could not make sense of them any more than he understood how the world spun, what drew her interest, the stories, her crazy stories. Sometimes she looked as if she wanted or needed something from him and he couldn't for the life of him guess what that might be.

.   .   .

"IF YOU DIE IN a dream, you die in real life," she said one day. "You just don't ever wake up." Her blue eyes were nothing remarkable but the blacks of them could glitter, like boot buttons. "Don't ever tell me you died in a nightmare."

Darby had no idea what to tell her. Her mouth hitched up to one side and the words fell out, that voice, a mixture of smoke and honey, and it was like a car wreck or something beautiful, something that could not be ignored, and she *had been* beautiful once.

She told him she and Adcock had driven naked one night, all the way to Redding, and Darby tried to see it, getting no farther than the road snaking under the trees. "Why do it? Why Redding?" he said.

She snorted. "Adcock said he didn't have the gas to make Shasta."

There were words for everything and mostly Darby tried to chase them down, trap them in corners. He was always somewhat out of breath.

"What," Harper said. "I have no idea what you could possibly be thinking. You have a face like I don't know."

Darby looked at her across the table, the rest of him off with the crew.

"For this sort of conversation," she said, "I'd just as soon stay at home."

More than anything, Harper liked to watch the planes. It was September. A few stinkpots chuffed along the lake and above, a sky a color Darby associated with hope, not the candy blue of summer but deeper.

She bent to the table, whispered like she didn't want anyone else to hear. "What do you think the story to that one is?"

Outside, a red Cessna banking over the lake. "Probably from Dinsmore," Darby ventured, stolid as ever, imagining only the short hop from there. He watched her face wince, close up, like a change purse. He'd kept company with some women in his time, a few, a good while back, and the memory offered no compass now. It'd always been about heat, not love or closeness, and when the candle had burned down, nothing remained. He thought there'd be all the time in the world for such matters. But her questions! He'd been the best sawyer who ever wore caulks in these woods. His family used to say the sap ran in their blood. They had another joke, something about the family tree, only Darby could never remember enough to tell it right.

Across the lake, the logging roads climbed the forested hills in diagonals. It'd be months until they pulled the pin in Cecilville.

"What do you dream about?" she asked. "How do you want to die?"

THEN THE IN-BETWEEN DAYS, Wednesday until next Tuesday. Darby owned a cabin in a narrow slot canyon, what he had to show for when there was still hell and money to be made in these woods. A looking-glass creek spilled under the trees. Steelhead massed this time of year, waiting on the fall rains, for the river to swell the banks so the fish could resume their impossible uphill swim, deeper in the mountains. He could watch the fish for hours, the glide in the beveled currents, their patience almost instructive.

It was Friday or Saturday when he sensed a difference in the piney air, like a sound he couldn't quite hear, and over the next days it changed, not a sound anymore, more a shape he couldn't make out. A Cooper's hawk circled high above one afternoon, the moon nosing over the treetops, the hawk's call cutting through the hills like the most sorrowful sound ever, and that *was* real. This other business—probably a dream stuck fast. And it was only then he thought of Harper, the claptrap and stories she'd fed him lately, and it suddenly made sense, reason enough at least to see or hear strange things. No doubt he'd be conducting seances by the time the boys returned.

He walked through the glade to the river, the moon throwing butter. In the wide tarn steelhead crowded and Darby watched the fish. A stirring from the depths, a steelhead rising, the moonlight glinting on its back, and it reminded him of the story about Harper. Everybody knew it, how Adcock supposedly had enjoyed standing her against a tree, outside their hideyhole, and flinging knives at her, a gypsy talent apparently picked up in prison. Darby wondered if she was naked when the knives came homing in, sticking the meat of the Doug fir, if that somehow raised the stakes for them.

A breeze pushed down the fall line, brisk and somehow old. Darby couldn't see himself motoring to Redding naked or anywhere else. He'd no trouble picturing Harper and Adcock, though. The water was a river of moonlight. Again the pitched call of the Cooper's hawk. And it felt like a place now, this *thing* he couldn't see or hear: ancient, buried deep.

A LITTLE BOY HAD DISAPPEARED in the Trinities that year and Harper was drawn to this, too. "Kids have been known to be sold into slavery," she told Darby, one of the unlikely accounts she cooked up to explain it. "Just because a thing's not supposed to happen doesn't mean that it won't."

The notices for the boy were tacked everywhere. The curtain of trees lining Route 3. The bulletin board of the cross-roads store that'd closed shop once the timber trade up and left. The door to the Forest Deli, closed as well. Frank, the kid's name was. Or maybe Jackie. The photos of him spooked Darby, the lost aspect in the boy's eyes, as if he knew his fate. In another way, though, he didn't seem gone at all, the hundreds of flyers flapping in the wind, like there were a battalion of Franks or Jackies in the forest.

Disappearances were a fact of the woods almost as much as the trees. The teenage girl hitching to Willow Creek a few years ago. The doper uncovered long after he went missing, shot to death, a chain around his neck. The woman up at Goldfield, her truck stuck fast in the snow, only the swollen creek talking.

But this particular kid—Harper's eyes flashed hungrily discussing it. Something was spiriting people away, she said.

"Maybe the trees. After all the years of cutting, the woods could be exacting its price. Like a toll."

She talked over his bum shoulder and he stole a peek behind, found only a mirror, that and Harper watching herself in it. A woman who looked like that in the Trinities: nothing else was expected of her. It was like a job and at one time Harper had been very good at it.

She wanted to know who'd miss a lost kid like that. "Who?" she said.

Surely the family, Darby allowed. Beyond that, relatives, friends.

Harper shook her head heavily. "Sometimes, no," she said.

An iffy afternoon, a sky like a tin ceiling. A craft tilted over the hills, the trees. Darby had been waiting for it all afternoon. He leaned in, mouth dipping into a flat smile, like a saucer. "That one there," he confided, indicating the high-wing job floating down to the airstrip. "Filled with Japanese gentlemen in for the bear hunt. All the way from Asia. Across the Pacific, you know, a bear's gallbladder is highly prized as an aphrodisiac."

Harper studied him, as if she might have missed something, and then a laugh like a small explosion springing from the middle of her, and it was as good as money to Darby and things opened up after that.

The next time at the Yellow Jacket she pulled out a pile of sepia-tinged photos as the sun slid behind the trees along the lake. It took him a few beats. A girl in a jumper, hair braided in ropes.

"Bet you were breaking hearts," he said, "even back in the third grade."

She asked what he was like—jug-eared or lumpy or big for his age.

"I was probably all those things at one time or other."

Few planes hazarded the mountains after dark. Someone lit the lights anyway and the ground shone. He tried to guess what it looked like, the cast and glow under the trees, so many trees. He'd never been in a plane. He wondered if it somehow seemed right to outlaw the woods from up there.

Lynette came out from the kitchen to share a smoke. "The job that never ends," she said. "Now I get to go home and cook." They kidded Darby about being the only game in town. "Just you, chief, among all us squaws," Lynette said. They talked about Davey—Lynette's husband, who lived weekdays in Yreka, his union job there—and then about their yellow-headed kids, the youngest of which, Libby, was still in grade school.

The sky above the treetops burned orange, a dying fire, and the turning happened so slowly, a slug's progress, that Darby almost didn't notice. He was beginning to look forward to their Tuesday afternoons.

AND THEN LYNETTE CLOSED the Yellow Jacket for the season. Harper and Darby found themselves outside in the almost-dark. She kept a dog named Ranger in her battered Chevy, a gentle black-and-white, and she let it out to do its business.

How was it October already? They stood awkward as distant cousins, unsure what to say. He heaved a stick for the dog and it hobbled off. From out on the road, notices for that Frank-or-Jackie kid flapped against the trunks, staring with dead eyes. Another end to something, his old life waiting for him back in his woods, a shirt that didn't quite fit anymore.

A truckful of orange-jacketed hunters banged through on 3, the bright colors dulled in the grain of twilight, and then nothing.

"You're not like the others," Harper said, words measured out slowly. Ranger toddled from the trees, deposited the stick, and waited. Her face: more shadow than face. Darby wished he could see all of it.

"No," he said. He had nothing to recommend him over the next, not looks or intelligence or qualities more elusive, such as general tallness or the capacity for dance. "I don't know anything about that."

Perhaps Lynette was watching from a darkened window, and if she was, what would she see? A man, a woman, and a dog. Nothing.

"You know, this doesn't have to stop," Harper said. "The afternoons. That nurse from public health—she'll be visiting either way."

Darby had not once asked after her kid, not the entire run of lunches. It shamed him, his gray face flushing. He tried to picture what sort of mother Harper might be but no picture came. And they heard it at first, one last plane lowering, trying to beat dark. Then, as if magic, the landing lights flicked on.

. . .

THEREAFTER ON TUESDAYS they took driving excursions and things veered to a new place.

They drove out to Lewiston, skipped stones from the trestle bridge over the green river. Up at the defunct Golden Jubilee mine, they explored the half-buried tailing carts, the outworn leach vats, the forest undergrowth rapidly reclaiming what had been. October, before the rains.

The truck engine pounded like mad and talk was virtually impossible. The green hills filled the windscreen like a movie.

Then one afternoon they drove up to the north end of the lake. Past the dredger pond and the tunnel of trees at Coffee Creek, the road opened up, a wide valley between walls of mountain. There'd been a village out here, once, submerged for decades after the dam went up, a place called Stringtown. In drought years, the gable of the Odd Fellows hall peeked above the edge of water like a ship's prow, other buildings, too, the Red and White store, the elementary school, the Whiskey Hill lodge, but this was not one of those years.

Darby spread a trapper blanket for them. The skin of lake wrinkled. Above, wedges of Canada geese beat to a warmer, if not better, place.

"Used to be a town here," he said and told her about it and then they sat quietly. He sipped from a thermos of sour coffee he'd brought along, offered Harper some and she waved it off.

Thin and filmy clouds pulled across like train cars shunted on a sidetrack. His hurt shoulder filled with needles and pins.

"Did you ever want to be anything?" he said. "Different than what you are, I mean."

"I know what you meant," she said. She wore a pile sweater, black with little dots on it like stars, and it suited her. She glanced over from the lake. "I thought I could be an actress. People told me I had the bearing. But that was a million years ago."

He closed his eyes, thought what it would be like to see Harper on a stage, her photo in a magazine.

"What about you?" she said.

"The sap runs in my blood," he said.

"There must have been something else."

She was gentler with him. Darby no longer flinched so much after he said things. He'd not been reminded of the boys at Cecilville for the longest time and he considered them now, what they'd say if they could see him here.

"I figured I might go fight in a war as a kid," he said. "See the world."

The air, keen and woody, blew out of the hills. He could sit like this forever. He felt nothing more than old, not the worst thing. Someday all that would remain would be the land. He waved an arm at the lake which spread flat and huge before them. "Everything's changing," he said.

Harper smoothed the blanket, pulled out the nub grass by her feet. "He had the loveliest singing voice," she said, gazing out over the water again. "A crooning sort of tenor. Could charm the birds from the trees. Must have been the Irish in him."

Darby waited for more but none came. Adcock hadn't run in his crowd, had worked the county roads—hot-patch detail, chip sealing—and he'd only known him in the way everybody knew everybody but he wasn't familiar with him. He knew about the throwing knives.

"I never told that to anyone," she said. "Funny, what stays with you."

A tired sun, pale and jaundiced, its feeble climb up the ladder of sky.

In the beginning, after Adcock left, after the ruined baby, she'd promise the crew of his imminent return and it became a joke told when she wasn't around, that they expected to see his sorry ass just about when the sawyers would be given back the woods.

It was on the drive home that Darby sensed the oddest feeling, a flurrying deep inside, like one tiny element had been added to the mix of a hundred or so in the universe, a difference that small, yet infinite, and he did not know what it was.

ALL OF THIS was at such a remove from the old days, the times before the boys packed off to Cecilville, when the gang used to make a night of it, drinking together, usually the Timbers, sometimes the Cedar Stock, or maybe the Bigfoot. Adcock's black presence had hung in the air always, like a fist or a warning. It'd been clear by then he wasn't returning but none of the tired loggers was up to trying anything even so.

The nights out were about drinking and forgetting. It

hardly mattered that in the last few years Harper's hair got spun with pewter. It was enough just being with her, the goosey hot feeling that *something* could happen at any moment—right there in the roadhouse, under the old growth, the tired prizefighters still going at it on the tube—although nothing ever did.

She was aware of what beat in their chests for her, relished taunting them with it. Late in the evenings, the lank hours of morning really, after all the stories and lies had been thrown out, the bottles drained of amber liquid, she'd kick her boots up on the battle-scarred bartop. "Fellas," she'd say, eyes squinted like sideways dimes. "They haven't yet invented the man who can handle the entirety of this woman."

The crew horselaughed, at all the right places, the ten or thirteen still left. When Harper was done, they let it go. Gradually the talk rounded back, the small points of discussion from before: speculation if the height of paper wasp nests in the trees portended big rains, the kokanee run in the East Fork.

"This ain't the whisky talking," she'd remind them, before last call, a voice jagged as a case of broken bottles.

And she stayed with Darby, the solitary drive back, his highbeams pushing away the dark, whatever else was out there. He hadn't been alone in that, so much time on their hands, all they had was time, a terrible thing.

A FEW DAYS LATER Darby found the old photos. The sun, a tardy riser now, inched over the lip of canyon, the fringe of trees. He'd taken to banking the fire before dropping off at night, shoving splits of green wood in the box so there'd still be spitting embers by morning.

His cabin had an upstairs room. An outdoor stairway led to it and a few years before Darby had built a landing under the branches, a place he liked to sit, up high enough in the air he was in the trees themselves, but his efforts had stopped at the storm door that opened to the inside. He had a mind now to swamp it out, remodel the room into a parlor. It smelled musty as a tomb. He cleaned out the crawl space behind the wall and under the roof beams, sweeping up the black rice of rodent droppings. In the tight corner, at the confluence of wall, roof and floor, he found a thumbed copy of *Ivanhoe* and he spent the rest of that day and the next reading it on the high perch in the branches. The story returned to him from so long ago, of Rowena and the disinherited knight, a shout fading across a great distance, and he tried to remember what it would be like to see a thing for the first time.

It was putting the book back that Darby uncovered the snapshots, about twenty of them, their finish faded to a coppery glaze. He thought at first they could have been there for ages, from the time before he owned the place. But on the back of one he found his Uncle Ted's name written in a blocky hand. The front side showed two fellows with flowing pappy beards, one of the pair presumably his great-uncle, them posing on springboard platforms with double-bitted axes, the springboards girding the massive base of a sequoia. In another, a crew labored with a drag saw, their chests thrust forward in exertion.

Others depicted loggers bucking a redwood for shingle bolts, a climber topping a spar tree, then the guy lines strung up to it.

Darby could not remember ever seeing them but they were of his people. He'd learned the family history from his father before the old man gave out his last. They'd come from Nova Scotia, the original bluenoses, and settled in a different woods, over a hundred miles west of the Trinities, the groves of giants, the coastal redwoods of Humboldt. Darby's grandfather had been a smoke boy shoveling coal on the main haul railroad that once trundled between the woods and the mill. A cousin on his mother's side had been a section hand, a gandy dancer who tamped down ties on the narrow-gauge track. Most of the family worked in the lumber camps along the Eel River, some of the enclaves now more ghost than town: Falk, McCloud, Larrabee, Hookton. A few had been the actual choppers, taming the tall forest with the long sweep of crosscut saws.

Darby flipped through the snapshots of the hardy men and wondered how his life might have been had not a labor strike descended from the trees, eventually driving his father east, over the coastal range. Cresting Weaver Bally, what the old man found must have seemed a younger version of the world, this rugged green country, the buckled hills, the few crossroad towns that had taken root under the old growth, a different woods altogether than that of the coast. A good place to get lost in. Perhaps this was what he'd wanted, somewhere the trees were plenty, the men few, the logging uphill and difficult but something, ultimately, he could call his own. It was wild country and had remained as such. Years later, the gyppo outfits Darby signed on with were essentially unchanged from his father's day: packs of hale men who toiled from the spring melt until winter hit again.

Darby had a brother, much older, who'd left the woods, hadn't caught word of him in twenty years, could be dead. He'd disappeared as much as any of those other people who'd vanished in the forest. Darby was the last of his line. There was no one else to tell the family tree joke to, to get it right.

He walked down the stairs and to the creek. The water ran thinner, the steelhead forming a cloud in the pool. And that place he'd seen from before, back in the days of the first lunches with Harper, that shape he couldn't quite make out—he could see it now. It was high in the mountains: a lodge, a tumbling river, a buck-and-rail fence stapling a pocket meadow, a scattering of outbuildings including the lodge within the rough oval of fencing.

And snow. Darby could identify that, too. He thought of the photos and it was possible this was a place he'd heard about, something his father might have said. But the Humboldt woods were one of rain, not snow.

The water dashed through the rocks, a mossy taste rising. A middling sun filtered through the trees. The steelhead looked about frozen in place, hardly alive. He sat on a boulder washed down in the overrun from the March squalls. There'd been so many places and trees and all of it harked back to

IN THE SNOW FOREST

another version of himself, a person he scarcely recognized. His father, in the very end, had lost grip on time and place and Darby wondered if the selfsame wasn't starting to occur to him.

But he had been there, this lodge in the high country meadow, the towering surround of ponderosas and Doug firs. He could even smell it, the woody green, like a thousand dangly car deodorizers, only better. He had been there and it seemed important and anything more he could not say.

THE NEXT TIME OUT he took Harper to the Hobel transfer site: to the dump. They had already been about everywhere there was to go. With the dump nearby, the afternoon wouldn't slip away so fast, a better destination anyway than it sounded. It was closed on Tuesdays and they had the run of it.

The transfer site amounted to five dumpsters and it was easy enough to look past them. The remnants of a brush pile smoked. Evergreens crowded the slopes and above tree line, the upthrust scarp of Sugar Pine Butte. Off in the distance, the clear-cuts on Slate Mountain stood out like a shaved head.

They sat close, the day frosty even with the sun. There were some dump bears, Mac and Mabel, that sometimes descended from the thick of forest and presently they appeared from behind the trunks, eyes slitted, an expression of surprise on their faces at finding anyone else on the premises. They rooted amidst the boxes without much interest, eventually shambling off, disappearing in the hang of smoke and trees.

A plane drew a line in the blue. Was it only two months of Tuesdays? Everything and nothing seemed to have happened in the time since.

"What are you thinking?" Harper said.

"I found some family photos a couple days ago," he told her. "It's been sneaking up on me." He held up his hands, as if they could fill in the rest.

Harper looked out her window. "Am I too old for you?" she said quietly. "Is that what it is?"

It took a while to catch her meaning. If anything he was the older one, though she couldn't have been too far behind. And then it broke clear, something he couldn't fully square even so. Adcock had been the love of Harper's life; anything that followed would only come up wanting.

"Never thought it my station," he said finally.

"Well, I wish you would," Harper said, turning back to him, the blue of her eyes dulled, like a galvanized bucket.

They made like two of the oldest teenagers, their ardor clumsy on the sprung bench seat. And when it was over, she brushed his head with her hand. "You ever take that thing off?" she said, indicating his watch cap.

He laughed at himself, how foolish he must have looked, bare-assed except for the knit cap.

"You're a sad sort of clown, aren't you?" she said, but softer, brushing his head again. "It's okay. I been with other kinds of clowns, you know."

A raft of cumulus floated in, the upper reaches taking on

the limited hues of a washrag. He tried to conjure the boys, the pines and firs toppling like toy soldiers, the tiny lifetime between when the saw cuts free and the tree hurtles to earth, but there was only the stuffy confines of the truck.

"I'm fat," Harper said. "You could upholster a chair with me."

"You're just right," Darby said.

"Could I still make a man look twice?"

He nodded.

"You're a good liar."

"I don't think so."

Her body had puckered a little, as anyone's would have. But it was not unlike gazing at a trick photo: He could see both what she'd been and what was coming for her and wasn't sure the future held a very pretty picture at all.

He had things he ached to say but no words to say them with, same old story, and he'd wearied of it. Feelings gathered in him, never went anywhere.

"It can't be easy," he said at last. "Your kid. A sickly child like that."

Harper leaned forward, poked at a split in the dash where stuffing had begun to boil out. "I'm unlucky," she said. "Some things you can change but luck isn't one of them." She shook out a smoke, cracked the window. "I used to have this dog. I'm speaking before my Ranger's time. Must be seven years ago by now. I don't know, seems I've always kept a dog."

A sudden gust rocked the pickup.

"This particular dog—a busy thing. Ran eight ways to trouble." She breathed a jet of smoke. "Wouldn't have made a very serviceable stock dog. It had spirit though and that's something."

"Dogs can be a unique comfort," Darby agreed.

"Funny that I can't think of its name offhand. Hector. I believe we called him Heck."

"Fine name for a dog," he said.

"What the Heck. It's coming back now. That was the joke we had—what the Heck."

He thought that was the end but Harper went on.

"Anyway, this one evening we were sitting out on the porch, having a civilized drink, whatnot, tall candle burning on a side table. Of course, Heck's nosing around where he shouldn't be. Next thing we know, his tail's caught fire. Must have backed into the candle. The dog dashes off, like he thinks he can outrun it. He just keeps running and running, the race of his life, I suppose. The most terrible smell of skin and hair. And Heck's just a red-hot blur by now, his sorry glow lighting up the night, the trees in the forest."

Harper hitched an eyebrow. "He just kept going. Never seen anything like it. When we finally caught up, there was nothing left. Nothing to show he'd ever been a dog."

She twiddled with the radio, a blast of static. Air leaked through the gap of window. "I don't even know why I told you that."

"It's a hard-luck story."

Her face was chapped from his heavy growth. "What the heck," she said.

Darby's heart thrilled yet from before. In the spotty light, the dump looked like the most beautiful place he'd ever seen. He'd secretly hoped that what they'd done, their tender rustlings, would be all he'd ever want from her but he was wrong in that. It was only the start. All week he had mulled over the kid, decided that it, the subject Harper never talked about, was the bridge that might close the distance between them. Now it was Adcock who hung in mind. Throughout her awful story, Darby couldn't help but see his troublesome presence and that somehow made it worse. He wondered what it would take to win a woman like Harper, what it would take to keep her.

Stray garbage wafted from a dumpster, kited on the wind, kept going.

"I'm not a very good person," she said evenly, staring out the front, a thousand-yard stare. "We can stop this right now."

"I trust you," he said.

In the dropping temperature their skin stippled with goose flesh. He could go again and even make a better job of it only it was time to leave.

Out on 3, the jitney that transported the handful of kids to the school way out in Weaverville made its slow progress homeward. Darby noticed Halloween decorations on a number of roadside trunks, the ghouls and goblins replacing the postings for that missing Frank-or-Jackie kid.

. . .

NOVEMBER. THE RAINS CAME. It didn't seem they'd ever, then they did.

Sometimes, at night, he'd wake, hear the crunch of footfalls in the duff. The cabin was so far from anything: probably only an animal. But in his sleep-hungry mind, he feared Adcock might be returning, making good on Harper's promise. Come morning, he would find only his familiar canyon and trees taking shape from the mist.

He thought about the lodge in the meadow, the old and buried-deep place he could see now, and it was like a balm. His aggrieved shoulder did not hurt so much, grew stronger each day. The trees were not so important. He felt like he was only now getting started, a wide river opening inside him.

IT WAS THE DUMP again the next Tuesday, an indistinct gray-green world on the other side of his streaky windows, a dirty ceiling of overcast sinking from tree line, a close dampness inside the cab.

He understood how to move, what was expected of him, but beyond that, he had no better idea than a barn swallow. It was only one afternoon a week, a couple of hours—that was all. And it was not so far off anymore, the crew's return. And where would Darby be then? Questions, everywhere questions! He held on to Harper with everything he had, hoped it was enough.

But this new place they'd reached: a door that only opened onto her sadness. There remained all the places closed to him.

Once their desperate thrashings ran their course, she wrapped herself in a somber quiet and it was all the more evident they came at these afternoons from different directions. And what Darby saw then was the smallness of his life. He'd never be daring. He could not throw knives or croon songs. But he could wait for her, like his steelhead in the currents, he could do that.

"I've spent half my life in bars," she told him, a hard, wistful edge to the words. She tucked a lock of hair behind an ear.

"You still have the rest of your life," Darby said.

"I guess that's what I'm afraid of."

He held her, the best he could do.

"Where did I find you?" she said.

The rain's temperature was only a couple of notches above snow. It pinged off the pickup's scabby hood. And past the drenched hills, he saw himself, out of the whisky nights, how he'd always been looking over someone else's shoulders at her. And now here he was and there was only Harper and even with all his doubts something wonderful ascended inside him, like a balloon. It was possible if he opened his mouth, it might float right out of him.

HE RAN INTO LYNETTE on a day more dripping than raining, down at the mailboxes by the store. As it turned out Davey still wasn't back from the union job in Yreka. And there'd been talk of reopening the Forest Deli.

"It won't be nowhere as good as the Yellow Jacket," he assured her.

Lynette smiled, the tiny void in it, a gap of teeth. She wasn't pretty in the way Harper was. Darby liked how freckles splashed across the bridge of her nose even so.

"A shame about Davey," he said.

"Oh, it's not the worst thing, is it? Sometimes I think Libby and her bunch miss him more than I do."

It seemed that was about it. There was one more thing, she said, a favor. Darby followed her on back, along 3, the trees receding on both sides of the two-lane at the dredger pond, bunching up again after Buckeye Creek.

The Yellow Jacket stood alone, shutters clapped, sign hanging off-kilter.

"Davey made that for me," Lynette said. "I would hate to lose it."

He pulled his truck close, clambered onto the hood, taking care with the cut-out shape of the wasp, the fine taper of its stinger. Lynette passed up whatever tools she had on hand, not the cleanest job, a socket wrench and lag bolts would've been more suitable, but it would keep, at least through winter.

"My hero," Lynette said once he slid down. And then, "I could probably scare up something in the kitchen."

Even with the lights burning, the inside remained dark. He winched up the shutter over the booth's window. Ridges and chop hitched along the lake. The sun struggled to make a show of it, a brightening rumor behind the gray. At the airfield, a wind sock tugging atop its high mooring.

From off in the kitchen Lynette called out, "I have soup. Nothing fancy. But it's free so the price is right."

Darby told her that would be fine.

She returned with two steaming bowls. They took opposite seats in the familiar booth. "So how's tricks?" she asked.

He shrugged. In the recess of his spoon he found a navy bean, a pinto bean, and noodles in the shapes of letters—M, V, O, and F.

"I'm not blind," Lynette said. "Tuesdays she still parks her Chevy here. Has to be seeing somebody." She stirred the broth, blew on it. "We're all adults. Your secret's safe with me, chief."

"It's good," Darby said, "the soup."

"I had nothing to do with it. Straight out of a can."

He dipped his spoon, the noodles failing to spell anything.

"I sometimes worry if I'm exciting enough," he said.

Lynette pulled her head back, as if she couldn't entirely fit him in frame. A scarf of overcast thickened on the hills. "You're a dear man, Darby. That has to count for something."

It sounded dainty, insufficient. After all Harper's years of roaring about, he amounted to a consolation prize, a stone that sank beneath the glowing prospects of life she'd once held. And there was still the matter with the kid. He didn't know from children, if he could care for one, let alone a child of such dire circumstances. Perhaps his affections only went so deep.

That burning dog came to mind, the story Harper had told, and it occurred to Darby he was not unlike it, nosing around where he shouldn't. "The details," he said. "They seem hard to work out."

"I think you want it perfect," Lynette said. "You got this thing in your head. How life should be. You keep convincing yourself you'll get in the game or whatever you call it. But you never do." She shook out pepper. "You're as young as you'll ever be. It's never easy. That's the best I can tell you."

He seemed to recall a rough patch, her and Davey, a number of years ago, and it had to be difficult yet, Davey miles and miles away.

It turned out there was one more favor. Her Libby was in a troop of girls; a nature walk had been scheduled, to earn them a commendation. "Davey promised to go," she said. "But with him still punching his card in Yreka . . . Supposed to be a man that goes along. For safety."

Darby agreed. A sorry affair, what the world was coming to, the need for a man to escort a brigade of girlies in the woods.

"How's Tuesday?" Lynette said. "So Harper can join us."

It was the day's fat middle when Darby pulled into his canyon. After two weeks of rain, the worst had blown out, the river up, running fast—he could hear its collective shout. Down at the banks he saw what he had missed in the river's recent froth and roil. It still rushed down but with less fervor. Amidst the white-dashed rapids, the side pool was again apparent, the green water clear to the bottom. Sometime, in the wake of the rains, the steelhead had moved on.

. . .

FOR A FEW DAYS, mild weather settled in, a memory of summer, a pause in the world swinging forward, the fresh-swept and deep skies. Come Tuesday, keener temperatures and wind had drifted back, but not the wet.

Darby was not fully prepared for the gaggle of uniformed girls, kneesocks pulled high on pipestem legs, acorn caps. He had told Harper only that they were doing Lynette a favor, had hoped being with the kids might chase her gloom, if only for a little while. He wanted to make her happy. If he could do that, maybe he could allow himself to want other things, too.

And it was like watching someone rouse from a bad sleep, her seeing the kids, a face that began with a question, then blooming into the wide creases of a grin. "Ha," she said, patting her hair. "I would have dressed a little nicer if I knew I'd have competition."

They waved to Lynette, the girls taking dull notice, then the lot of them set out along the trail that skirted the Trinity. The water chuckled through river rock, deadfall stacked on the gravel bar from the recent high water.

Darby saw Lynette's Libby, a kid pale as milk with yellow hair, and he remembered as well the photo Harper had shown him back in the beginning, the little girl version of herself with ropy braids.

They allowed the knot of girls and Lynette to put distance between them, Lynette admonishing the kids to stick together. Light filtered through the branches and there didn't seem to be anything sinister lurking in the woods, only this aggregate of girls with knees knobby as fists.

The kids sang a song about a sailor heading to sea. It started up one end, got picked up by others, ripples in the melody, and it spun this way. From fifty yards back, he could not catch all the words yet it felt like a singalong recited back in his day, an ancient song.

"So where do you want to go?" Harper asked. "Everybody has a sailor in his heart itching to go to sea."

"It's only a kid's song," Darby said.

She bobbed her head, indicating the girls with her nose. "What, you think recklessness is only a good idea when you're young? If I could, I'd be gone faster than you could say Jackie Robinson."

She told him she had three destinations she aimed to get to before it was all said and done. One was Crescent City, which, but for the prison that once housed Adcock, wasn't really anywhere, over the coastal range to the ocean and due north. Another was farther north, in Washington, Willapa Bay, home of the oldest stands of Doug fir. "They have four-leaf clovers big as daisies. I have the brochure and everything." The kids moved on to another song, one Darby couldn't call up, it filled with mysterious hand slaps and arm waving. "How about you?" she asked.

"There's this place," he said. Darby could fix it on the map now, the lodge in the meadow, had been there back in his first days of logging, high above where the broadleaf forest gave way, a woods that had none of the green density of the madrones, chinquapins, and bays, the growth of the lowlands, only the open stands of giant conifers able to defy the legendary snows. "The weather comes down," he said, "like the machine up in the clouds was broken. A snowpack that remains into June, sometimes July."

The lodge had been built by a moneyed fellow well over a half century ago. He'd been in the gravel business, owned the contract that paved Los Angeles, and had taken the profits, run so far and high that no road could ever reach him. "It was designed by a famous lady architect of the day," Darby said, the whole works constructed of incense cedar, the bark peeled, logs treated, then the bark put back on. "Teddy Roosevelt himself stayed there. The Rough Rider." Somehow the land had fallen to the forest service.

"It's up there," he said, waving at Billy's Peak. "I don't know. A man who gives up what he loves for a thing he loves even more. It says something to me."

He was lost enough in their conversation that he didn't see the group had stopped and almost walked up their backs.

"Girls," Lynette said, "we're lucky to have with us one of the most skilled woodsmen ever. I'm sure Darby has a number of things to share."

He thought the deal was to just escort the kids. Lynette had already commented on ponderosas, their puzzle bark. He could've talked about the steelhead but with them long gone from his creek, it didn't feel so significant anymore. "I'll tell you something my father told to me," he said at last.

"*Louder*," hooted the chubby girl with the neat bob of hair.

He cleared out his throat, started again. "You got your evergreens and most people can't tell one from the other. It's like they're all the same. But I got a secret to identification." He paused, all those pebble eyes on him. Through the trees, the Trinity tumbled fast, clean. "It's in the needles. A pine falls in packets. A fir's are flat. Spruce come in spirals." He stooped to retrieve some from the duff, his knees cracking like sticks of wood themselves. He held out his hand. "You see. Pine—packets. Fir—flat. Spruce—spirals. You can use the letters in order to remember."

It felt like a speech to him and once Darby had stated it, his face reddened. He could have said more, about each type of timber, the methods used to fell and yard them, wedges and skidders and spar trees, but all that would occur to him later that night. Now his voice trailed off into embarrassment and he feared he'd not made any sense at all.

The group tramped along the trail, Harper and Darby straggling.

"You did good," Harper said. "Bully for you."

Up ahead, Darby noticed kids kneeling to find their own samples, correcting each other, voices pitched like songbirds. The sun was a lemon over the trees and for a few moments he sensed a warm ease inside him, like a coiled rope unspooling. The kids weren't holding hands anymore, had grown prankish, ducking behind trunks to scare each other. He hoped Lynette might ask him to talk again and he could tell them something else.

Three of the girls dawdled behind until they were only ten feet in front of Darby and Harper. They whispered, then the tall girl, the one with a port-wine stain on her neck, turned and asked, "Do you have kids?"

"No," he told them.

They turned to Harper and asked.

She hooked her arm in the crook of Darby's. "How do you like my Boy Scout?" Harper said.

They giggled, scurried up to the rest, the mirth passed from one side to the other the way their sailor song had. Another peeled off, a strip of a thing with owlish glasses. "Is he your boyfriend?" the girl said, nasal as a clarinet, then didn't wait for an answer, ran back, the group stealing looks behind.

By the time they'd completed the circle of trail, dark had swooped in like a big-winged bird. They sang a farewell, shouted goodbyes, calling Harper and Darby by their first names, as if they were now part of their troop.

A good day, he thought later. He leaned against the railing on his high deck in the branches. Above, stars sparked and glowed: the sweep of night sky. His steelhead were gone but this afternoon was something new. He dropped off to sleep up there and wove a variation of the day, neither Lynette nor Harper in it, only the girls, and strangest yet, Darby was Adcock somehow, not fearsome or throwing knives, but gentle Adcock singing among the little girls.

He awoke in dead night under the jittering stars. For a few moments he could not place where he was or even who. The unsettling but not unpleasant dream faded. And it occurred to him that Harper had never told her third destination.

IT WOULD BE ANOTHER MONTH, Darby figured, until the boys clattered home from Cecilville, his sawyer instincts sensing what lay beyond the rubble of mountains, three thousand miles of snow. In the meantime, northerlies rocked the windows, winds airmailed from the top of the world.

Sometimes he still trudged down to the creek, the currents no longer spuming or high on the banks. The tarn that had once held his steelhead held only an emerald cast, a scattering of river rock. He envied the fish, their rootless lives. All his days, Darby had viewed the world in the vertical lean of trees and now there was more.

His shoulder mended, the ball meshing cleanly with socket, and somewhere, deeper inside, he felt himself mending, too, a wound that had been there a long time, perhaps forever.

The days were meager candles, each one shorter than the last.

And he felt oddly lucky even though he couldn't claim to say how the vagaries of fortune worked. Three months ago he'd been the unluckiest man in the Trinities, unable to go with the rest, the last hurrah. Now he could see past the woods and Harper had been the reason for a lot of that, but not all.

He thought he caught a glimpse of Adcock's Scout one day on an errand to Lewiston. It could have been manzanita, what he saw as he barreled past the forest service trail, the same pale money-green. He doubled back after a mile of mulling it over and found nothing.

THEN, ABOUT THE TIME November got torn off the calendar for good, Harper started to visit Darby at his cabin. It was not a Tuesday. He heard the rasp of her Chevy floating up the dish of land, through his trees, and believed it at first to be only the wash of river, and he remained with the task at hand, up a tall ladder, applying chinking to the side of the cabin that took the weather.

Harper swung out from the car as if it was the most natural thing. "So this is where you live," she called up, her mouth set, that gashed smile. She wore the pile sweater with the dots like stars. She told him county public health would be stopping over now more frequently and what settled in mind as she said this was *time,* how his weeks would no longer have to revolve around the few hours of a single afternoon, a selfish consideration.

She asked what a girl had to do to get the cook's tour and Darby showed her the run of the cabin, the four squat rooms on the first floor. "I been meaning to muck all this out," he told her, opening the storm door on the second-story landing. "Could make another bedroom out of it," he said. "You never know."

He dragged a couple of chairs onto his high perch. He had some apples in the larder, tart greenies, and he sliced them up, the wedges, except for one or two, uneaten, browning on the plate.

A brisk noon but sunny. For a while they conversed and he thought Harper had climbed out of whatever hollow she'd languished in these past weeks. Maybe the afternoon with the girls had been just the right medicine.

But the swell of mood didn't hold. The talk eventually ran dry and in the absence of anything to say he could see her sliding down, her sorrow once again a wall that they were on opposite sides of. Harper quieted, her head lolling on her shoulders. "I could fall asleep right now," she said.

"I've been dreaming myself recently," Darby said, hopefully. "I hadn't for the longest time. Now I wake up and my head is full of them."

Her unexpected visit—he'd imagined a day like this, like a dream itself.

"It's good to see you," he said.

Harper moved so slowly, as if under water. He wanted to reach out, to gather her in.

Only later that night did he fully weigh what the nurse's added house calls had to mean. Darby had seen the kid only once, a number of years ago, back when the crossroads store was still plying its trade, when Adcock was still around. Harper standing over the assorted liquor bottles, the kid slung across her hip, the freakish hump like a shark swimming in the middle of its back. He had heard around that it hadn't been given a bantam's chance to outlast the year.

In the coming days, Harper returned to Darby's canyon,

each visit the same story, a flicker of humor at the outset, her fire, then that giving way, fading. Maybe if she could talk about it, it might help. He would be there, whenever she was ready.

December. The air brittle as a fossil, cold enough for snow. He should have been busy running errands, laying in supplies. Instead Darby kept to the property for fear of missing Harper. By now the nurse was making house calls almost daily.

And then one day, he failed to hear the clank of the Chevy climbing the rutted trail. He'd been upcanyon, in a grove, taking measure on a tanoak snag he'd had designs on. If he was lucky, it'd yield a cord, maybe more.

It was on the way back—his heart athrum, the notion of firing up his saw, the cavitating wail tearing a hole in the day— that he saw Harper. She was off at a hundred yards' distance in a pocket clearing. He was about to halloo through the trees but he hung back.

She stood, frozen, head canted to one side, like a statue, or a scarecrow, and at first Darby thought she must have spotted his Cooper's hawk circling in the halo of sky except he found nothing above save for a dingy batting of clouds. From somewhere the memory of Adcock surfaced, the game of throwing knives, and it must have been like this, Harper transfixed, the blade on its terrible flight toward her. Or maybe, he thought, it wasn't the knives at all but Harper listening to his lilting tenor in the white noise of wind and river.

She stood beyond all reason, Darby himself frozen now,

spying her through the thicket. And so it went. He could not guess how long it continued, the sight chilling him and yet he could not stop watching.

In time, Adcock's ugly presence vanished and it was only Harper. And it was as if Darby's eyes could see through her, past her clothes, under skin and blood, down to where impulse and purpose beat, the very center. She was on the edge of something, had to stand that still or she might miss it, lose the possibility forever. Even across that distance, through the trees, the low wattage of sun, there was the hard silver of her eyes, her damaged beauty.

And then, ever so gradually, Harper unloosed herself from the spot, the feeling flown, a settled expression. She tucked herself into the front of the car, drove off. And indeed when she visited next, a couple days on, her face did appear settled, as if something had been decided. She'd lost weight in the recent weeks, her cheekbones angling the way they once had, slackness gone. She wore the same boots the boys wore, lace-ups with fat soles, except she was not one of them. She smelled of citrus and soap. He wanted to tell her things, so much he wanted.

He took her down to the creek, pointed out where the steelhead had gathered, their speckly dorsals, the majestic glide in the tarn. "One day they swum on," he said. "During the rains. But it was a gift, to have them here."

"I swear," she told him. "The way you study this river. You'd think it was an RCA or something."

Harper put her hand in the cup of his. They sat on the

boulder along the bank, her hand small as a child's but roughened, nicked from the years.

"That place you mentioned. The lodge in the snow."

"The Stengel lodge," he said, the name of the long-ago gravel contractor.

"I've been thinking about it. That and all the lost people. The kid on the trees. Maybe that's where they are. Maybe they're not really lost at all." She cut her eyes. "It makes a pleasant thought, doesn't it?"

The water pulsed, a hushed roar, like distant traffic, and they had to call out over it to be sufficiently heard.

"I have to go to town," Harper said. "For a few days."

"Is everything okay?" Darby said and only after the words had left him did he realize he'd been searching how to ask such a question ever since the beginning, and now it had come, easy as the currents spilling down.

She considered him as she might the very old or very young: indulgently. "I'll be back," she said.

After she left, the Chevy bumping down the furrowed trail, Darby retrieved his saw from the back of the pumphouse where it lay all these months, and had at the snag of tanoak. And once the blade was stilled, the tree bucked, ready to be split, the air no longer ringing with its clamorous whine—it was then he saw he was on the edge of a decision himself.

HE MADE FOR THE HIGH COUNTRY on a mid-December day, under a socked-in sky. Only one road climbed up there, a conveyance that had once served the gold mines and the timber outfits after that. During cutting season, especially fall, a steady traffic of rigs used to descend the corkscrew, studded with fir and pine, on the way to the mills.

More recently, the logging road had fallen to disuse and the elements. It banded the Trinity, notched into the side of the mountain, little more than a single lane. At times the spillway was hundreds of feet below, a roiling braid of water and riprap at the other end of the big swallow of air.

As Darby left the low-lying forest behind, the close palings of broadleafs giving way to airy stands of conifers, he rose into snow country, the road itself becoming a slurry of white, remnants of the November rains that had dropped flakes on high. The driving bogged down until it was like navigating a greased cookie tin. He pulled off where a culvert thrust out of the roadway like a busted finger, and ditched the truck under an alder. From there, he would snowshoe overland, retracing a side creek which drained into the river.

He had been there before, back when he was young and green, as sawyers go, but it was clear even then he could interpret trees the way some could the scripture. It'd been on a gyppo contract tighter than catgut and they'd got well caught in it. The snows had come early, the blanket of white falling all the way down to the valley, the outfit still owing thousands of board feet. They did their level best to make a go of it, nearly did, but a nasty storm skirled through before Thanksgiving, leaving a wall of snow. There'd been nothing to do but to tell the crews to hang up their caulks for the season.

One of the bull bucks had recruited Darby and another fellow, a seasoned sawyer named Hennessey, to slog in, salvage what they could. "Afraid it'll be the armstrong method, boys," the buck had told them. "Hand labor and whatnot." He promised they'd draw enough to board with Aunt Polly until the melt. Darby would've gone anyway, relished the idea, cutting in the manner of those who'd come before, the stories his father had told.

All that seemed like distant history. Hennessey had come to grief years ago, ages before the bottom had dropped out of the timber trade. Most of the rest had moved on, the few that remained up at Cecilville.

There was only a few feet of drifted snow now, nothing like that time. Below and behind Darby, the valley came in and out of the low ceiling of fog, his snowshoes pressing webbed prints in the untracked white. He carried a pack and it bit into his bad shoulder but nothing he couldn't manage. The river tumbled down like a hermit's beard.

In that particular year, he and Hennessey had constructed a pulk, a sledge of enormous scale designed to carry their equipment and provisions. Hennessey had logged in British Columbia and he knew of such a transport. They'd knocked it together with both care and haste, shaping two strips of fir into narrow guide runners, pounding planks atop these for a platform, fashioning a cover from a tarp of duck canvas. They'd tramped out front of it like two draft horses, pulling the whole deal with rigid traces.

It had been miles until the bridge, and Darby could recall the feeling yet, the near-mythical wonder of cresting the ridge-line, finding the trestled span of wood and steel in such rugged country, a monument to the gravel contractor, the last of his road engineering know-how. It was dark when he and Hennessey finally reached the scoop of meadow. It had looked like pieces of the moon falling, snow painting the air, the lodge itself clad in a hill of white, glint of ice in the tall trees, the spiked picket of mountains.

Darby could see the memory like a snow globe he could hold in hand. There was no sound now other than the muffle of footfalls, the chuffing of breath. He had the strange sensation of snowshoeing both forward and back at the same time, into the hills of white, into his own history.

And he slogged onward. He thought he'd glimpse the bridge anytime now, through the snow-tufted branches. All he found, however, was the surging river and the unbroken wilderness. He snowshoed for miles. For a distance he trod in another set of footprints, made some time before, the cupped tracks filled with newer snow, a wide depression like the person might have dragged an object alongside. After a while, the tracks gave out, disappearing in the drifts, no answer to who owned them. And then it was only Darby and the chevrons of deer hooves in the white, the even marks of a kit fox cutting across his path to the river. In the crook of a fir branch a flapping crow observed his heavy progress.

But still no bridge.

He and Hennessey had rifled the door to the lodge and camped inside, the storm kicking up again, the confetti of snow dropping as it had the last of that fall. Most of the first floor was a great hall, a hearth at one end composed of granite rock. The second floor contained a warren of chambers, sleeping quarters and porches and sitting parlors. In the rooms to the back, snow had piled over the windows, a wall of crystal on the other side of glass, a disturbing sense of being entombed in an iceberg. They'd built a snapping fire in the maw of hearth, dragging in wind- and deadfall, sometimes levering an entire trunk in, the fire eating it all like a pencil in a sharpener. In the warming air, shelves of snow slid off the roof, a thump like a body falling.

The logging had been as difficult as any he'd had, the crusted white at times reaching up to his neck, Darby and Hennessey toiling in silence. There was a generator shack in the meadow, its pelton wheel rusted fast, the last of its electricity spun fifty years back. Off near the distant line of forest lay the hull of an outmoded earth-moving vehicle which must have been airlifted piece by piece over the gray tusks of mountain.

Nights in the lodge Darby had roamed the maze of rooms, the winter air hiding in corners, like children. The place had been scoured clean, the only remnants from what had been a few framed photos on a hallway wall, the contents of each dissolving from the years. A nag with a three-piece rowboat broken down into sections along the sway of its back. A grouping of three kids showing a skein of fish, smiles bright as lightbulbs. The last photo, the oddest of the lot, was snapped a few years after, the kids older, the horse laid out on the ground, apparently dead, a wreath of flowers resting on its crown, the kids grieving.

He and Hennessey had remained with the appointed task at hand until the food ran out, the days by then having lost their names and numbers. In the end, they broke up the massive sledge for firewood, leaving the downed trunks until the other end of winter.

Now, Darby's pack dug into his shoulders. The stillness of the snow forest was entire. Dusk gained on spry legs, the dimming of that hour. He snowshoed, reaching a section of river that tumbled in a waterfall.

He unloosed his pack, laid out the bivvy sack it contained, crouched alongside the water that pooled on the downstream side of the falls. It was troubling, the fact of the Stengel lodge, lost in the creases of hill and time. But he had been there. He could see all of it now and that was sufficient. He set about to make a fire and, once it took, mended it with branches from the slash of a ponderosa. In the going light, the temperature dove.

The falls hurtled. There was a shadow in the pool and it remained, despite the absence of sun, and now it moved and Darby noticed that it was not a shadow at all but fish: an immense crowd of steelhead in the deep water. They stirred under the wavelets, a city of fish. He climbed up the rocks at the mouth of the falls and looked down on them. The angry water rushed, the spray freezing into ice, falling away in the manner he imagined stars died.

He had the feeling that all his life had led him to this sharp promontory. The creek in his slot canyon was a part of the same river system. It was possible that his steelhead might be among the mass below, that he could have ridden their backs to get here.

Eventually, he climbed down, cooked a modest meal over the flames, his insides still quickened as before. He bedded down along the pool and the magic fish, the star-pocked heavens above. When he woke the next morning, the steelhead were gone. A clear day. Darby had no opinion whether the fish had continued on, past the impossible thirty-foot vault of water and rock. Or whether this was indeed the spawning pool they'd swum uphill to reach and now they had let gravity carry them back. He bent down to the water, thrust his head under, as if that could tell him something. The crushing cold staggered him, his hair turning to strands of ice after reemerging.

He tried hard to arrive at some sort of reckoning. He considered the journey of the fish, from this high point in the snow forest, the downhill run to the ocean through the waterways that emptied out of Humboldt, the rivers Darby could tick off like a six-fingered hand: the Van Duzen, Salmon, Mad, Trinity, Klamath, and Eel, where his people had dug in and made a life.

He had not thought of Harper for the longest time and now he did. Near the end of his old man's days, his father had lost his purchase on the present, a feebleness of mind after the final stroke, and Darby had cared for him like a mother. He had been a difficult man and this end came as a kind of grace. His hard ways softened. If there were any tender moments of their lives together, it was this time that Darby thought of, the family stories his father had told him, his only grasp on who he was, where he'd come from.

Darby mulled over if it might be similar with Harper and her kid, the rewards in the limited confines of such a relationship. It was possible to love an unwhole person—this he understood. He had done it before.

It was afternoon when he quit the camp, following his tracks from yesterday. On the way out, he sighted a plane, high in the blue, waggling over the crags, gauging what snowpack there was. He reclaimed his pickup under the alder where he'd left it. And Darby could see all the way down to the valley, the distance foreshortening, autumn still holding. It was only winter in the high country.

ON HIS RETURN, his cabin seemed small—the box that had contained him all these years. The moon was a constant companion, a ghosted shape in the day, as if too tired in the ebbing year to rise and set.

Darby split the tanoak snag that he had dropped earlier and the activity fired him. He was strong, better, his body renewing itself, a feeling like sugar in his bones. It would be any day now that the boys would be back from Cecilville, winter headed for the Trinities like an oncoming train. Time—a cruel joke. Before fall, all he had was time. Now it ran through his hands like water. So much ground to cover before the crew returned.

The crunch of the maul striking log rang out through the trees. He thought about Harper and the kid, wondering about their visit to town, what it could mean. He could do more with regards to the kid. He knew that now.

It grew wintry and he kept at it until the last round was split. The wind pressed down from the hills, carrying in its wide arms the green smells of the snow forest. He had been there and now there were other places to consider.

HARPER WOULD VISIT DARBY once more up at his cabin.

He had been ready and waiting and when the Chevy's hack wafted up the canyon it struck his ears like a familiar melody. She looked thin and tired but happy to see him. She told him a joke about a dog and a cigar and he laughed even though he didn't get all of it.

"I thought of you," he said. "How you were doing. In town and all."

Her mouth jerked, starting to say something, but she didn't. "I can't stay long today," she told him finally. "But I'm here with you now."

He got a fire going in an oil drum down by the creek. When the flames leveled, he put chicken over it, russet potatoes at the fire's edge. The smells of his cooking rose. The sun hit only the tops of the trees these days, everything else shadow.

"My mother used to say you couldn't trust a man who cooks," Harper said. "But I think she was just answering for my father's shortcomings."

When they were done, Darby put their plates in the river, let the water wash over them, the currents a soft clap of green water. He unfolded his trapper blanket. His fingers worked the buttons of her flannel shirt. If he could have crawled inside it and stayed, he would have. They moved together, a slow rhythm, Harper above, the branches waving like arms.

"I'm not used to doing this with you without a steering wheel poking in my back," she said once they were done. She looked off, across the water, the moss growing on the wall of granite on the opposite bank. "You are the most romantic man I have ever known," she told him. "You don't have too much competition in that category. But there it is."

He thought about the snow forest, all that he had to tell her, the fact of him walking across the frozen ribs of winter. He had done it for himself but now it felt as if he'd somehow done it for her, too—for both of them. He had walked away from his old life, from one side and out the other, and now there was everything that he could see ahead of him, dim but there.

It was chilly and yet not so bad under the scratchy blanket, the heat of their skin. Darby thought about her kid again. He would ask about the situation. That was where he could start. His father had liked playing with a flashlight, toward the end, the glimmer of its beam on the walls, and he wondered if such a thing might carry a similar draw for the kid. He would move closer and closer, like stepping-stones across a river, until there was no distance between him and Harper, until they were on the same side. First, before all that, he showed her the pictures he'd unearthed in his cabin, of men and trees, showed her the photo of his great-uncle Ted.

Harper studied it with interest. "You favor your uncle," she said after a time, putting the print alongside Darby's face.

He considered the snapshot but couldn't see it. "He's dead, I guess."

"Well, then I suppose I picked the right one of you."

Time to go, she told him, just like that. They sorted out their clothes, pulled them on, walked under the trees to her Chevy.

"I was just getting started," he said.

She looked up at him from the front seat of her auto, a face clouding over, deciding something. She reached for his hand, took it, held it close to her mouth and Darby thought she might bite it, but she kissed him instead. He remembered sticking his head in the icy water. He heard the static of his river and in that, the notes of its music, and it stopped him for a moment. Back as a kid, he had played piano, taken lessons in it, a ramshackle spinet that sat in the sun parlor, the last key of which stuck. He could not say from where the memory had issued, only that he had played the piano, not well, and it seemed significant.

"What?" Harper said.

"I can tell you later."

"I was thinking," she said, then stopped.

Darby waited for more.

"Maybe you would come up to my place. Next time, I mean." She told him the day, her face troubling all the while, voice tailing off high like a girl's.

He fairly trembled as the words came tripping out. He had not made it to the Stengels' outpost in the snow forest. But this: this was a new place and he would get to go there. His life was changing. He could feel the very ticking of it.

"That would suit me," he said, "down to the floor. It really would."

In the intervening days, he dreamed a swirl of images, of Adcock and Harper, them pulling their misshapen kid around in a Radio Flyer, of that burning dog. Other things, too: Darby and Harper and a little girl apparently of their own making, her name seemingly Nicky or maybe something fancy like Jenny Greer. Nerves, he told himself. He had waited so long. He could wait a bit longer.

SHE MET HIM out front of her place the day of the visit, a nose red from the chill, like she had stood out there for a while. Darby had not been up that particular road to One-Eyed Ridge, a thin band curving and climbing under the green. He had expected a neglected house, the absence of a man's hand, but it proved far worse. The shack leaning to one side, glass broken out of windows, newspaper stuffed in the mullions to keep out the weather. The roof gapped in places. Somebody had tacked tin up there trying to effect some sort of repair, at the peak, but it'd blown off, secured by a few last screws, the piece beating against the side of the house. Adcock's Scout out front, on rusted wheels, weedy saplings growing through a vent, the car looking like it hadn't been operable for ages, only a mouse house now, her dog Ranger sniffing around the stove-in side of it.

Harper stood tall, as if she could blot out the ugly truth, her afflicted shack. She had an embarrassed air and something else Darby couldn't read.

"I brought you some tanoak," he told her, gesturing back toward the pickup sitting heavy with the face cord he'd trucked up. "For keeping Mr. Frost from your door."

He couldn't see how a woman might get in all the wood for winter and from appearances he wasn't off the mark, a woodpile down to splinters, the bones of furniture in the yard suggesting she'd been breaking that up to burn.

Darby went off to deck and stack the cord. He remembered the stories of knives and surveyed the trunks for a blade-stuck pattern, a profile that might conform to her shape, but found nothing. He had cast about what to bring the kid, guessing what such a child might want, finally landing on a puppet he'd fashioned from soft pine, strung together with twine, a lumberjack with an ax in hand, the handle of which was a toothpick, a flat stone for the axhead. He'd left it on the seat of the truck, wrapped in paper.

Harper joined him on the side of house when he was done, eyes rimmed, skin around them swollen. She rubbed her arms, outside in only shirtsleeves. Darby took off his coat and wrapped it around her.

He thought she'd ask him in, but she didn't. They conversed dully. It felt like snow, they agreed.

"Any day now," Darby said.

Probably the kid was sleeping. A little bobble of wet hung from the end of Harper's nose. She wondered if Lynette's troop of apple-kneed girls would be caroling at the knot of houses around the lake, if it was something they could go along on as well. "Do kids still do that sort of thing?" she said.

He had imagined how this day might play out, ever since Harper had extended the invitation. They could get a fire going inside from the tanoak. The kid would be playing with the puppet in a corner. A cozy picture he'd warmed himself with. And then he would tell her everything he had been thinking.

He leaned on the wood now. It was different from what he'd imagined. He took her mood for shame; after all the talk, the whisky bravado, this was what her life came to. It didn't matter. What mattered was all that lay ahead.

"There is something I have to say," Darby began. He was not good with words but he used the ones he had. He explained what the last few months had meant. "It was like I was lost before then," he said. At first, he had fought this new feeling, had gotten comfortable in his pitiful ways, had thought he was too old for love, that love like tackle football or chicken pox was a young man's game, and it was a long, long time since he'd been that young. He told her, too, where his people had come from, the life he had rediscovered and how all of it, in some way, was connected. After all these years of waiting, it took the fish to rouse him. If she'd join him, they could follow their progress down the river, out to the raggedy tin edge of the Pacific, get a shot at a regular life. It wasn't too late. Surely, somebody in Humboldt would recognize the family name. Perhaps he could hook on at the mills, get a starter home in the company town of Forestville. He'd still be working timber, as a trimmerman or manning the head rig. If it all worked they could consider another child. They could wait out the winter, leave in spring, when the blooms of Henderson's shooting stars began thrusting upward.

"I'm prepared to love and care for your child like it was my own," he said. "I can do that. It is something I want to do."

Harper watched him, her swollen eyes, a stricken look, face screwing into itself. He did not know what to make of it, feared his words thudded wide. He'd seen romance scenes at the picture shows, a swell of strings surging, how the woman's face on the screen often failed to register the emotion which beat inside, how love could assume other masks, and maybe that was the situation now.

She held up a hand, a cop stopping traffic, and Darby did stop. For a few moments, she just stared, her blank eyes. "Did you hear that?" she said.

He did not hear anything.

Harper strode around the house to the front, up the steps. He followed. She opened the door and he was below so he couldn't glimpse inside.

"Oh, look at the baby," she said, little hop of a gasp, as if the kid might have done a clever trick. He thought of the puppet, still on the front bench of his truck, him eager to present it.

It was only when he reached the top step that Darby could see over Harper's shoulder, what she'd meant. *Oh, look at the baby.* The little kid lying on the floor, a plastic grocery sack over its head, the room as mean as the outdoors, trash stacked over. He took it in, like food, regarding it intently, trying to get it clear in his head, that sorry little kid, its legs blue like it had been there for some time.

And then he turned, sat on the broken stoop. Below the trees on the ridgeline, the accordion folds of hill fell away. Strands of woodsmoke rose from the habitations down there. He thought he could see the lake, far down, through the trunks but maybe not. The trees on the other side of the road tilted in the same direction as the shack.

Harper sat next to him.

"I'm unlucky," she said and then said all that she had not the last four and some months, all that Darby had wondered over, what was wrong with the kid. There were words Darby didn't know, medical-sounding, and couldn't have been anything good. She had loved it the best she could. Some of that amounted to hoping for the worst, betting on death, a terrible thing. "You can't know," she said and Darby nodded that he could not. "I thought maybe this once." She swung her head. "I don't know what I thought."

There was more, about what the recent visit to town entailed, how the end was supposed to happen then, what the doctors had predicted, except the kid had hung on. She was only helping it in the direction it was headed. "Love can be a burden," she told him. "Sometimes more than a person can carry." Gradually all Darby heard was a roaring in his ears, like a river at flood stage. And what he'd remember long after was the kid in those shorty pants, a room far too cold for such attire, and that told him all he needed.

"What you said," Harper said. "It can still be that way. Doesn't have to change a thing." And then, "I'm not sure they'd have believed just me. It's a better story with you here. I hoped to make more a show of it, though."

The wind spun down off of Billy's Peak. He thought he heard the faint notes of a song, of singing.

"I would have wanted it any way except for this," he said. "I was looking forward to meeting the kid."

They sat that way for a while, the door to the shack open, knocking against a table.

"I'll go to town," he said. "Tell them only how we found the kid. An accident—that's what I'll tell them."

"You can tell them anything you want," Harper said.

"That's what I'll tell them."

"I know," she said.

There was nothing else for him to say and he got up, walked to the truck. Harper on the steps with her dog, the flung-open door behind her.

Darby would not remember much from the fifty-mile drive. Along the way he tossed the puppet. All those years of banking on luck or nature, for somebody or -thing to snatch the kid away, like that Frank-or-Jackie boy on the trees, only it never happened. Part of Darby could see her now, waiting on the authorities, rehearsing what to say, the actress she once ached to be. Mostly, though, he could see that it had taken him, the fact of Darby in her life, to do this, a kind of love, although a form of it he could do nothing with.

He told the sheriff what he had promised and when he was done he remained in town, a left front tire throwing thread that he'd been meaning to replace. It snowed the next day, flakes the size of underwear and socks, all the weather he'd sensed since the boys lit out for Cecilville, a three-day blizzard locking up the roads between town and home. When it cleared, he had the feeling the crew would be back and Harper gone and when he returned to his slot canyon, he found a note written in pencil, the two words on it already wearing away: *Couldn't wait.*

YEARS PASSED, the world spinning forward on its rusty hinges.

It wasn't the same after the boys came home. They met a number of times at the Timbers, tried to rekindle their fraternity but the snap had gone out, Harper, no doubt, the glue that'd kept it intact. They knew of his discovering the child at Harper's but nothing else, not their time together in the months of that fall, and that was okay with Darby. It was his own.

There would be modest timber jobs from time to time, nothing again approaching the scope of Cecilville. A handful of the crew moved on. There were only a few left. Despite his plans, Darby stayed in the slot canyon. He built a bridge that arced like a question mark over his creek, to watch the steelhead every autumn, the magic fish in his water.

Sometimes he thought of Harper, whether she ever made it to that third destination of hers, the one she'd never told of. Other times he thought she might have caught up with Adcock and it gladdened him some. He wanted her to be happy. She deserved that at least. And then, over time, he thought of her less and less until she scarcely came to mind anymore.

Strangely, every year he grew more hopeful and what started out as a tiny flame back in that fall now crackled inside him like the Biblical bush. He marveled over the intricate piecework of love, how it moved not in thunderclaps, but countless little triggers. One morning, he awoke and remembered the family tree joke. For the few moments of sleep seeping out of him he could see the whole string of it, and he laughed aloud, and then it passed beyond his grasp again as he climbed to full wakefulness.

And then one spring, a body washed down Swift Creek, a girl no more than eleven who'd apparently gone missing.

Lynette's Davey found her. He'd taken his dredge up to the hills on a Saturday, searching for gold in the rocks. Darby asked him about it afterwards, asked until he could imagine it was *he* who'd made the unfortunate discovery.

He drove out to Swift Creek, the oxbow of river that Davey had told him. A handsome day, all the different variations of greens, the first blooms dotting the dogwoods. There would have been a splash upstream. Then some gray above the water, then more. At first it must have seemed like a steelhead, the biggest in the history of the world. Then the rest of it would become evident as it carried down the fall line of river. Darby would have had to wade in to pull her out, a blind attempt to rescue a girl long beyond saving, the body cold and wet and of the river.

Nobody had claimed her. After all the years of the woods taking people, now it was throwing one back. They pasted a likeness of the child on milk cartons, which was new, from Weaverville up to Callahan, a sea of milk. And still her identity was a mystery.

Darby stood watching the water, the mesmerizing pulse, Swift Creek fat with the spring melt. He was closer to death than birth; he could sense the heavy tug of it sometimes. And he mourned all that had been and would no longer be, the parts of his life that reached out from him like branches, mourned a little girl whose name the world would never know.

MENNO'S
GRANDDAUGHTER

I t rained the year Lindsay turned forty, in the beginning and then clear through spring, so that the year never properly sorted itself out, and now it was fall again, October turning into November, the creaky music of tree frogs heralding the coming wet.

She'd lived in the west half her life, under the upthrust of sequoias, the far north of California altogether different from the Hudson Valley where she'd grown up. It was years since she'd returned, so many she could almost believe the Hudson Valley was something half-remembered from a book. Tomorrow Lindsay would rattle off in her Nash, under the trees and over the coastal range to Redding, where she'd catch the 2:00 A.M. *Cascade*, the first in a series of trains that would trundle eastward and back.

Her bags were packed, standing neatly in the mudroom, like soldiers awaiting orders. Her parents were getting on and that was the reason for the visit, seeing to the needs of encroaching age and infirmity. It was normal to be anxious though the family reunion was only part of it. Lindsay felt as if she was going backwards in some unforeseen way, the works thrown into reverse. It felt like dangerous terrain, best left unexplored.

She was old enough for things to have happened. For the

world to have torn itself down to its stuffing, then pieced itself back together. To have been married, once, and to lose the man twice, to divorce and then death. She never met Whit's second wife. But to the world, the one that read books or knew of such matters, Lindsay would always be his wife.

She had made mistakes, like anybody, had been knocked about by life. But Lindsay was still young, halfway down to the bottom of the pocket perhaps, but young and still girlish and pretty, her beauty something she came by as naturally as a flower. Her smile was slightly skewed and her teeth not perfect and her voice so deep it sounded as if it issued from a well—hearing Lindsay on the telephone, one might mistake her for a fat person. It all worked in an unfussed-over way, though in truth she'd little use for her looks, her only concession to vanity the infrequent purchase of a hat.

So tomorrow she'd board the first leg of a hopscotch route of rails that would carry her across the country—up to Seattle, east through Idaho and Montana, south into Wyoming, a dead run to Chicago, from where she would travel in more straightforward fashion to New York. Lindsay had never been to Wyoming. That was where Whit ran when he left her, to the Bighorns, the first time she lost him. She'd no idea if the second wife still lived there, but it seemed somehow important to see the place, to take its measure, if only from a speeding train.

THE *CASCADE* WAS STILL MILES OFF, working up the funnel of valley, the beam of its locomotive scouring the dark. A small number of people milled about the station platform; off to the side, a knot of Southern Pacific employees talking and glancing toward the northbound train, waiting to restock the club and diner cars, their final detail before punching out.

There was the sense of a few souls awake in a sleeping world and, too, a Christmas Eve sort of anticipation, like Lindsay was off to meet someone, a mysterious stranger perhaps.

Nearby was a woman with two small children, a boy and a girl, the little ones slumped on a duffel shaped like a squashed tuber. "I don't think that train's moving at all," the woman said.

It did seem possible that the train could be frozen on the tracks, off in the distance.

"They look like angels," Lindsay said of the children, which, in the sketchy halo of light, wasn't so far off the mark.

"Not a care in the world," the woman said. "That's the myth, isn't it? A happy childhood." She had a wide face and eyeglasses shaped like cat eyes.

From out on the street, voices: last call and closing time at the avenue bar, the Engine Number 9. She and Whit had been there once, back when the establishment operated under a different name. A car started up and backfired, the ample shape of a Packard slowly rolling down the street. It honked at the looming streamliner, now fast approaching the platform.

The *Cascade* pulled into the station, a hiss of brakes, an apron of steam gathered about the trucked wheels.

"Here we go," the mother said. "All aboard."

The train was longer than a city building was tall, the two-tone gray livery of the Pullman cars like a shadow overlaid on the night. A dark-skinned porter whose face reminded Lindsay of that baseball-playing fellow conveyed her bags to her roomette.

The accommodations were snug as a womb, scarcely big enough to contain them both, a sink and toilet shoehorned in the tight dimensions. When the porter folded down the wide seat, the room was more bed than room. He indicated a cupboard along the wall which he could access from the hallway. If she stowed her shoes within, they'd be dutifully shined by morning. The diner was closed but he could scare up something from the club car. Lindsay said that wouldn't be necessary and he retreated, drawing the doorway curtains, the snap of the compartment door latching shut.

Once pulling loose of Redding, the train climbed a trestle bridge over the Pit River, into the hills. Lindsay was too tired for sleep. She lay in her bedclothes, idly considering the expense. She didn't want for money. A distant uncle had left her some and Whit had unaccountably, too.

The sky carried the last of a waning hunter's moon. In the deep cleft of the Sacramento River Canyon, the earth fell away. After Mount Shasta hulked into view, the streamliner hit straighter track, marshaling its speed, the even side-to-side of train burnishing rail gradually lulling Lindsay to sleep. She roused hours later to the repeated melody of three notes: a member of the wait staff passing through the Pullman, sounding chimes in the corridor to announce breakfast service.

Outside, the train was traveling the tented peaks of the Cascade Range from which it took its name. Green conifers petered out at timberline, a ruff of snow above that. Seeing the hills encased in white, she had a waking jolt that she slept clear into winter, the streamliner having jumped the tracks, still plowing north.

DOWN AT THE FAR END of the diner car, waiters smoothly one-stepped around the pantry, retrieving bread and butter and other finishing details of their service. The vermeil silverware of the empty place setting across from Lindsay gleamed bright as electricity. The car was mostly empty and the utter civility and starched linen appointments felt like a show put on for her benefit.

A waiter appeared at her elbow to whisk away what remained of her apple pancakes and ask if there might be anything else. The train chattered along the downgrade to Odell Lake.

"If it's no trouble," Lindsay said, "a pen and paper."

He told her very good, as if the exact answer he'd hoped for, returning briskly to present both items with a flourish. Two children bounced stagger-legged down the length of the rocking car, laughing, turning at the pantry, then back up toward Lindsay. It was the same two from last night, from the station platform in Redding. The train hit a patch of rough track just as they were about to run past and they lurched into Lindsay's table, sending the vase of cut flowers wobbling like a duckpin.

"Evan and Sarah Jane!" The woman with the cat-eye glass-es strode up to collect the children.

"It's all right," Lindsay assured her.

"Oh, hello again," the woman said. "It's you."

The boy, Lindsay could see, was the older of the two but not by much more than a year—Irish twins they used to call it. The girl had a bit of the mother in her broad features.

"You'll get us thrown off the train," the woman told them. "They won't even stop. They'll just toss us off." She laughed and turned to Lindsay. "I have to love them. I have no other choice in the matter."

"Such a fine gentleman and lady," Lindsay said, then pulled a face for the children. She could do a chipmunk and another like a lizard.

"Their first time on a train," the woman confided. "We're off to the folks up in Corvallis. It's the first time for a lot of things." She gazed at the pair, but softer, like she was maybe recalling a rag end of memory from when she was their age, some private, little piece of excitement from back then.

"I'm on my way to visit my parents, too," Lindsay offered.

The woman nodded and waited as if there might have been more. But what else was there to say? That her mother was impossible, disagreeable as piss and colder than hail? Lindsay could not remember a single kind word, only pointless stories about long-dead relatives that seemed to go on forever. Her father had enjoyed the balance of her affections, though later Lindsay decided that his kindness masked a timidness for life that she feared might be somehow hereditary. She had a sister somewhere back there, too, a couple of years older, and Lindsay couldn't abide her any better than her parents. One could certainly fly these days—it was 1957, after all—but Lindsay was in no rush to get back there.

"It's back east," she told the woman. "I'm taking enough trains to become a conductor myself." She smiled, put her hand in front of her mouth to cover her teeth, an old habit, and left it at that, as if all the different carrier lines and states were too much to go into.

There was a river outside the window. The land had opened up and the snow was behind them, in the steeps of the Cascades. The river ran white and fast, collecting green in the oxbows. Lindsay remembered what Whit used to say about snow, that it was luck, though earlier it hadn't felt like that.

"This is pretty country," the woman said. She nodded at her fidgeting charges. "They're too young to appreciate beauty. It's lost on them. Or maybe everything is beautiful or an adventure and they can't tell the difference. I think you have to actually lose something to know what it's really worth."

Lindsay swiveled around from the window and tried to figure what the woman might have lost.

"Pretty," the woman said. "Look at me: the philosopher."

The three remained in the aisle, as if standing for a portrait. Children were something of a mystery to Lindsay. It would take a miracle of a romantic and biological nature at her age for such a possibility. It was still fair enough to wonder. She guessed the woman was thirty. She used to try to guess about Whit's second wife, like a parlor game, what she might have looked like, her interests. Lindsay couldn't see her with cat-eye glasses. She had a hard time picturing her at all, never able to develop any concrete idea of what sort of woman would steal another woman's husband.

Up front, in the galley beyond the pantry, the clang of pots and pans, breakfast preparation moving into lunch.

"Well," the woman said and took this as a cue to usher the children out of the diner car, leaving Lindsay alone with a blank sheet of paper bearing the Southern Pacific crest at the top.

The smell of the little ones lingered—milk and sugar. She herself had been that young though it seemed impossible.

The train entered a tunnel, then blasted back into daylight, the tracks descending into a valley. Lindsay uncapped the pen. *Dear Whit, I can just hear you declaring this journey a fine adventure on the high iron.*

In her crabbed Palmer cursive she told of the trip thus far, motoring over the coastal range to Redding, the fall colors, the pink of the dogwoods like the lipstick the bad girls in high school used to wear. She had paid close attention, as if the last time she might be seeing all of it. But now the steady rhythm of the *Cascade* relaxed her and with each new mile her fears for the trip seemed unfounded, only nonsense and foolishness.

SHE CHANGED TRAIN LINES in Seattle and, too, the stationery on which she continued her letter to Whit, the pages bearing the mountain goat insignia of the Great Northern. Puget Sound flashed by the observation lounge: ferries churning water, the great tonnage of oceangoing vessels steaming slowly out to sea. *There are sea lions, more like dogs with flippers if you ask me. One in particular, Whit, an impish pup, reminded me of Kenai.*

At Stevens Pass, Lindsay spotted snow, her second sighting in as many days. The Skykomish shot through its bends, the rapids jetting like water from a firehose. Bald eagles wheeled and patrolled the gravel banks. Maybe it had been something like this for Whit, following a trail of words, one after the other, not quite understanding where it all would lead.

When she glanced up from her writing, it came as more than a small skip-beat of surprise to find Whit staring at her: his photo from the back of the dust jacket to *Night Voyage*, the fellow opposite her in the lounge cradling the book in his arms.

The man lowered the cover. "You look as if you've seen a ghost," he told her. A long-drawn face, blued from shaving stubble. He tugged on an ear and said, "It's a darn good read."

"I'm familiar with it," Lindsay said.

"It's not my first time," he said. "The book, I mean." He told her he was an engineer. "Not the kind that drives a train," he said and smiled as if it was a joke he was supposed to say. His name was Atlee. He worked on hydroelectric dams throughout the west and spoke with animation, using words like "corker" and "ginger peachy."

The solarium roof carried the firefly glow of late afternoon. From the dome Lindsay could see the articulated line of the *Empire Builder* ascending track, the overhang of peaks like the jawbone and teeth of some enormous and extinct animal.

In the approaching rock wall, the opening to a tunnel.

Atlee craned around. "That's one of the longest bores in existence," he said. "Almost eight miles long." In the false night of the tunnel, the lights were lit. Atlee explained that dams and tunnels weren't so different. He was trying to impress, Lindsay could see, and she enjoyed the attention. "Listen to me," he said, stretching his legs. "*I* must be the longest bore in existence."

"No, it's remarkable," Lindsay said. "It's so—" What she thought of then wasn't trains or tunnels but how Whit used to make sport of her shyness, her inability to ask strangers—even policemen—for directions. It amused him at first and, in the way these things often slid, later became one more jagged edge of irritation. "It's their job," he would say about policemen. "Besides, a pretty woman like you. It makes their day."

Lindsay smoothed the fabric of her dress. The air seemed charged—glittery—deep in the embrace of rock. She'd observed that older men were attracted to her these days, as if an invisible line had been crossed, and she didn't know how she felt about that.

"It's only that people take the train all the time," she said at last. "Never give it a second thought, the workings of it, just treat it like it's one more force of nature, like a river or a tree."

"I couldn't agree more," Atlee told her. He leaned forward in the high-backed club chair. Lindsay had no idea what he saw when he looked at her. She had a scattering of gray hair—and an invasion of rogue hairs in other places that she now had to keep after.

She wondered if the train might be burrowing toward the earth's middle. It felt like a spell, in the tunnel, like all the normal rules weren't working. She consulted her watch to see if the second hand was still sweeping around the circle of numbers and it was.

She smiled at Atlee. Inside her: it was like machinery waking up, parts of her slowly clanking to life, shaking rust off. Atlee was tall. She'd always been drawn like gravity to tall men.

Then the *Empire Builder* clacked out the eastward nostril of tunnel and the mood broke and they were just two strangers on a train. Lindsay felt flushed. Maybe she was coming down with something.

Atlee remained hunched forward in his seat. He was a nice man—she could see that. But that queasy, unnamed fear again, flapping in her ribs, a caged bird.

"Excuse me," Lindsay said abruptly. "I must be going." She swept up her letter and made an unsteady exit out the dome-liner, up to her compartment in one of the forward sleeper cars.

IN SPOKANE THE TRAIN SAT at the terminal while a railroad crew meshed cars in and cut others out from the *Empire Builder*'s consist. Outside her compartment window she could see a car knocker slinking along the track, peering under the train, searching for God only knew what. Baggagemen hoisted luggage and slung it into the hold. Beyond the station, the streetlamps of town, a trolley mounting a hump of hill.

Once the streamliner began rolling again, she walked the length of the train, back to the observation car, which was half full and dark as a nightclub, the wall sconces amber and glowing invitingly. The man from before, the engineer named Atlee, was where she'd left him under the dome, quite possibly there since the afternoon although it appeared he'd shaved since and the copy of *Night Voyage* was nowhere in evidence.

He rose when he saw Lindsay, a small smile riding his boxy face.

"I must not have my sea legs yet," Lindsay apologized. She realized she'd not yet told him her name and so she did, but nothing else.

Atlee laughed, a yapping dog's bark. "It's just the coincidence," he said. "The same last name from the book I was reading."

They sat together on a couch, its leather creased, comfortable as an old wallet. In the muted light, the Indian designs on the bulkhead and curtains were colorful but not so garish.

Atlee asked her if she cared for a cocktail. "A highball would be the item," he said. "That's train lingo. Highball."

The whisky bit at the back of her throat, not an altogether unpleasant sensation. They sat and sipped their drinks, the train rocketing through the darkened prairie flats.

"Do you travel much?" Lindsay asked. "Your line of work."

"It comes with the territory," Atlee said, then asked how about her.

"I used to," she told him. "That was another life, as the saying goes."

"To other lives, then," Atlee said. He lifted his glass, studied the contents, then tipped it back.

It occurred to Lindsay he might not be as old as she originally thought. Even with its long hang, she liked his face. She asked if he'd ever been to Gatchell.

"Wyoming?" he said. "In fact, I have. I don't know what I can tell you. It's in the Bighorns. Not much of a place. The roads are red, paved with crushed clinker rock. The damnedest thing. But Gatchell—blink and you'll miss it. I think the singular big event is when the train pulls into town."

Above, through the domed window, the night-rushing sky, the spin of stars and planets. It would always be mystery, what had come of Whit, an untold secret. He'd met someone else, run off with her, later died—enough said. But why Gatchell? Lindsay had seen it on a map. In two days' time, it would briefly fill the rectangle of a train window, the faintest hope that that might tell her more. At least she would see it and that was something.

Atlee cleared his throat, rattled the ice in the bottom of his highball. From the far end of the car Lindsay overheard a woman saying, "Oh no, not his glasses." Someone else answered, "Yes, he's blind without them." And then the first voice repeating, "Oh no."

She could hear a whistle and off in the distance the sight of a freight train racing in the night, a nearly endless string of reefer and gondola and hopper cars, like charms of a bracelet.

Lindsay nestled closer. "Talking is often overrated," she said. "Don't you think?"

"Most times I'd rather read than talk," Atlee agreed. "Present company excluded, of course." He extended his free arm to signal the barkeep. His jauntiness from the afternoon was mostly gone, the bit of it that remained not enough to veil a sadness. Lindsay decided she liked him better this way.

With the second drink downed, she reached for his hand, interlacing their fingers, the skin of his palm leathery, scuffed as a glove. "Cozy," she said. "There's something about night."

He smelled of liniment, a tang of cologne. She could feel the solidness of his arms—arms that had done work and still carried the memory.

"I used to be afraid to talk to strangers," she said.

Atlee smiled his downcast smile, hummed the refrain from a song she couldn't quite place. And the thought arrived like something that had been fixed on the landscape all along and Lindsay was only now near enough to perceive its shape.

"I have a roomette," she told Atlee. "It's really quite nice."

SHE FORGOT ABOUT THE LETTER, about leaving it out on the table in her compartment, and this was what Atlee noticed when he sat on the edge of her berth, the page with the engraved Southern Pacific crest at the top and Whit's name

inked underneath. Lindsay watched his face close up, as if trying to compute a difficult math problem and having no luck.

"Yes," she told him. "I am. Or I was."

"I don't understand," Atlee said.

She lifted his arm by the wrist. "Do you remember that
other life I mentioned?"

For a while, they occupied themselves with each other. It
had been long enough since her last time that Lindsay hoped
everything was proceeding according to Hoyle. They became a
knot of arms and legs, rocking up and down with the *Empire
Builder*, part of the streamliner themselves. Atlee grunted a bit
and then shortly they were done and afterward they lay side by
side atop the bedding. There was the uncomfortable presence
of Whit in the roomette. She wondered if his affair had started
along a similar collision of happenstance and desire. Lindsay
couldn't even recall the woman's name anymore, only that it
could have been a man's name. She thought it began with the
letter A: Avery perhaps.

"Forgive me," Atlee said. "I'm just submarined over here."
His voice: small and faraway. "The odds must be astronomical.
The very book I'm reading."

The Pullman canted, the train taking a bend in track, then
gradually righting itself.

"I remember when he wrote it," Lindsay said.

Atlee lifted himself on an elbow. "What happened to
him?" he asked. "I mean, why?"

"He used to say a lot of a good thing isn't much more of a

good thing." Lindsay worried a chipped nail with a finger. "I never really understood that."

His agent had phoned that day, to relay the news, and later the wire services had contacted her, inquiring if she could explain any better the circumstances. What else could she add? A gun was involved: he killed himself—that was all Lindsay had been told; what little else there was she would learn from newspaper accounts. Whit had gone to ground after running off to the Bighorns: no more books, nothing, only silence. "Perhaps you should ask his other wife," she'd suggested to the callers, but what she'd really wanted to say was, "It wasn't during my watch."

Atlee scratched himself thoughtfully.

"The world never loved him enough," Lindsay said quietly. "Or at least not in the way he wanted or needed."

She could see Atlee working on this, the ratcheting of cams and lifters and gears in his head, all the machinery that might break the information down so that it could be digested. And what Lindsay felt then was bad. There were holes in people, voids, the inner landscape an unmappable world. One could only get so far and even then it was, at best, conjecture.

"He was—" Atlee began to say. "He was a great writer."

"Yes," Lindsay said. "Obviously that wasn't enough."

His teeth chattered and she wrapped the end of the blanket around him. She leaned over and parted the blinds to peek out, saw a cottonwood in a field, the tree empty of leaves, only gnarled limbs, scraggy as a wraith. She saw a buck fence extending miles but no animals within its compass.

"What was he like?" Atlee said, his voice smaller yet.

Stories she could tell him. Whit had hit her, toward the end, hit her and ripped her things, family albums and dresses, and worse yet she'd felt somehow responsible, as if she'd some fundamental lack that deserved his rage. Even though the suspicion had flown in the years since, its imprint remained.

"He was a big man," she said. He had chased grizzlies across the frozen reach of the Brooks Range and lived to write about it, and this was the Whit she would breathe life into. She crossed her arms over her chest, for modesty, then lowered them, deciding instead she liked Atlee's eyes roaming her body.

"This was when we were still married," she said. "What I'm going to tell you. He used to enjoy a drink. That's known, I guess."

"I'd heard that," Atlee said.

"Yes, not all one hears is true. But that was at least. He could find a reason to celebrate. It was a talent—five days until spring, two days after New Year's, the last of the Thanksgiving leftovers. We were still young or not old enough to be sensible. We thought nothing could hurt us. Invincible."

She could hear the toot of a whistle, the *Empire Builder* perhaps signaling another train out on the open prairie. She felt like a smoke, had given up the habit years before, but remembering stirred her, the nights at the roadhouse out by a bend in the Eel. There used to be loggers throwing horseshoes in a pit outside, all night long the ring of men pitching iron. It reminded Lindsay of a bell in a prizefight, the start of a round.

"We were celebrating for some reason," she said.

"Five days until spring," Atlee offered.

"Maybe." It occurred to Lindsay that early in an evening drink filled one with possibilities and later, after midnight, it was the opposite.

"Whit left the bar for some reason," she said. "It might have been to play horseshoes or just visit the bathroom. I was left talking to this fellow named Ed. Everybody knew me and I knew everybody. This must have been fall, the end of cutting season."

"Okay," Atlee said.

"I knew Ed was sweet on me. He'd tell me I had the nicest legs. He said if Whit weren't in the picture, he'd like to be. I thought it was only smart talk. He was a tiny man, no bigger than a boy. He had a beard and it made him look like one of Santa's elves. I thought it was just Ed trying to feel bigger than who he was."

Atlee hitched onto his side, the blanket falling away. His eyes were hungry but not for Lindsay. It was what she was telling him.

"I could see it coming," she said. "Ed edging over, me backing up. Like a dance. I didn't want to believe it was happening except he kept coming, lips screwing up to kiss me."

"What did you do?" Atlee said.

"I pushed him back. At that point, Whit returned from wherever. He didn't see anything. It's all normal for a while. But then this Ed business began to eat at me. Not so much what he'd done, but because he did it with Whit so nearby. I couldn't venture what he was thinking. In the end it all seemed more directed at Whit than me."

"Did you tell him?" Atlee said.

Lindsay shook her head. "Not at first." She closed her eyes, could see Ed at the bar with the rest, daring her to tell, betting on the fact she wouldn't.

"Then what?"

"I told Whit."

The highballs were slowly wearing off. She thought about the woman with the cat-eye glasses from the *Cascade*, the reunion with her folks in Corvallis, could see them sitting around a big table, plates of steaming food, the way it was supposed to be. Lindsay suddenly felt tired, so tired. She flicked on the reading lamp, then back off. In the corridor of the Pullman, hushed voices and footsteps and the door at the end of the car sliding open and shut. Atlee swallowed, waiting for her to continue.

"There's not much more to it," she said. She told him how Whit did not immediately fly upon the man. An apology was all he wanted. "For the lady," he'd said. The timber crew was a hardy lot as these things went, but only a fool would have stood up to Whit and everybody except for Ed knew that. The little man launched into a tirade. When he got excited, he stuttered and it was difficult in the beginning to make out much of what he said, mostly a torrent of stuck consonants and flecks of spittle. Then it came clearer. It was about Whit, running him down, so much hate, a lifetime of being small. "You don't treat the lady right," Ed stammered. "Anybody with eyes can see that. It'll be over in a year."

Whit allowed the banty to finish his piece. Then he spoke so softly, all the rough-and-tumble men in the roadhouse had to lean in to hear. "An apology won't make you a smaller man," he'd said. "It won't make you five foot one. It won't make you four-eleven." He paused and then said louder, "You'll still be *five foot three.*"

Atlee's face wore a satisfied expression. People preferred to think of Whit this way: wild, unpredictable as a rogue gust of wind. Alive.

"Well," Lindsay said. "The rest is what you might expect. Whit lifted Ed right onto the bartop." The logger had looked so small up there, like an object you might put on a dashboard. There'd been a certain aspect to the room, that *something* was going to happen, an awful sense of the air sucking itself out of the place. Even Ed appeared like this was what he wanted all along, to be put in his place, to be shoved back down. Then the crush of Whit's fist and Ed's nose and then Ed tumbling backwards, over the bar and onto the floor, the clinking of bottles breaking the fall.

"A barfight's not John Wayne," Lindsay said. "One punch and it's over." She stared at Atlee. "That's what I can tell you about my husband."

Atlee pushed a hand across his face. "It's a known fact," he said, "that people often envy the famous."

The train rolled over smooth track. Lindsay thought about

what she didn't tell, that as wrong as Ed was, he'd been right about one thing: his timetable for the end of the marriage. It must have been in the air, along with everything else, must have been like an animal on dodgy legs at that point, something Lindsay and Whit knew but weren't admitting yet or maybe only Lindsay wasn't. Even so, Whit had sprung to her—and their—defense, an awful and hard thing, like fighting against himself and Ed. He had done that. He'd done terrible things to her. But he had done this for her, too.

Lindsay could feel Atlee leaving even before he reached for his clothes. Her life with Whit had transformed her; she'd become like a character in one of his books, knowable but not entirely real. She wondered if Atlee had ever done this before, met a woman on a train in this manner, and decided probably not. He appeared lonely. She tried to conjure a life for him and all she could come up with was solitary meals in diners with names like the Busy Bee. This was an event in his life.

"Ed was a horse's ass," Atlee said, standing up from the bed. "You are a beautiful woman, though."

"If that's true," Lindsay said, "it's not as if it's any of my doing."

Atlee bowed slightly. With his lanky features and gloomy bearing he reminded her of a church deacon. After he backed out from the roomette, she wrapped the blanket over herself and watched the fields of longstem grass waving in pale moonlight like water. Montana. Tomorrow she would board a feeder line that would trace a sickle shape into northern Wyoming:

Clearmont, Buffalo, the Powder River basin, and, eventually, the Bighorns and Gatchell. She would see where Whit had run. She'd thought that it would be no more than attaching a picture to a name, a momentary glimpse as the train whistled past the crossing. *This is where Whit retrieved his mail. Over there, he bought his ink and paper. There: the dive bar he'd sneak off to afternoons to bend elbows with the 4:00 P.M. regulars.*

In all that, she had not much considered the second wife and now she did. Lindsay could always remain on the *Empire Builder*, follow a different path to Chicago. But she felt herself being pulled to Wyoming, pulled by something more powerful than the trio of Alco PA diesels at the nose of the streamliner, and she'd the uncomfortable sense she was helpless to stop it.

LINDSAY WOKE AT DAWN, sweaty and a taste of chalk in her mouth, suspecting at first it was the whisky from the night before. At Whitefish she quit the *Empire Builder* and sat for hours at the depot, awaiting the arrival of the branch carrier, nodding off on a wooden bench, eavesdropping, when she was awake, to the slow commerce behind the cage of the ticket window. A vagrant stumbled into the dusty hall, carrying on a noisy quarrel with himself until a train official shooed him. She replayed the events of the evening before with Atlee and had no opinion on it either way.

The train finally arrived before noon, her Pullman bearing the name *Roaring Camp* in gold leaf across the rolling stock's letterboard, the roomette a frowzy imitation of her prior accommodations, the walls constructed of metal and grained to resemble wood veneer. She settled in her compartment, happy at least to be moving again.

OVER THE NEXT HOURS, fever bloomed in Lindsay, her throat turning pebbly and coated, and she thought if she could just lie still the ague might fly off as quietly as it had descended.

She roused midafternoon to a bell ringing at a station. The train churned past a main drag of one-story buildings— city hall, a tavern called the Hub, another, the Bum's Retreat— then tight rows of gable-and-wing houses.

Farther out from the town grid, Lindsay saw two boys huddled around the open hood of a Chevy pickup, staring intently at its innards. She watched a squat cattle dog running behind a fence, for a distance giving the train good chase. Dark masses of Angus grazed in fields of yellowing grass. On the horizon were saddlebacked hills but closer in it was the unrelieved monotony of open country, everywhere the sky pressing down. She felt exposed out here, nowhere to hide, only an occasional house in the yawning distance, the rest treeless high plains.

LINDSAY DID NOT GET BETTER.

The fever climbed. Time became unreliable. Her head filled with the traffic of odd thoughts.

When she was nine her class was assigned a composition about the revolutionary era in American history. Every day after school Lindsay had pedaled her bicycle to the stone-pillared

Carnegie library, where she labored until almost dark, researching her own particular topic of interest, Washington's crossing of the Delaware, and then the long glide under the tunnel of elms and home. She was a studious girl. She collected butterflies. Sometimes she helped with her father's stamps. She took long solitary walks with her dog in the neighbor's field.

That week, however, there was only the composition, the heroic passage across the icy currents. She finished days before it was due, attached the neat pages in a blue binder, and placed the report in her locker at school.

Lindsay shared the locker with a girl named Patsy Burgess. They were rivals of sorts, although Lindsay suspected the rivalry was mostly one-sided. Patsy, for her part, didn't seem to know Lindsay existed. She was in the most advanced reading group in the class and could play circles around Lindsay on the clarinet. Sometimes Lindsay thought she might want to be Patsy Burgess.

The reports were duly collected and then days of anxious waiting and then after lunch the next week Lindsay saw the stack of them on a table in the front of the classroom, her blue cover among them. She waited, through endless long-division exercises, the scratch of pencil jottings.

When it was time, her teacher stood before the class. Mrs. Chalmers was a tall, heavyset woman with a powdered face. She smelled of lavender and something less pleasant underneath—earthy and close. She announced Lindsay's name. "There is a word, Lindsay," Mrs. Chalmers said, "for when you take someone else's ideas and claim them as your own. It might seem nothing. But it is a form of stealing."

Lindsay listened to the reproach but did not understand. She'd spent days at the library, consulting various dusty encyclopedias and compendiums. She'd read about Washington's teeth, which were wooden.

"Patsy wrote a very similar composition," Mrs. Chalmers said. "How do you care to explain that?"

There was a rushing in Lindsay's head that drowned out what words she might have, and what words were there anyway?

"No?" Mrs. Chalmers said. "I didn't think so. You'll have to write the composition again, Lindsay. This time be certain it's your own."

After class let out, Lindsay approached Mrs. Chalmers and tried to tell her of the week's research in the library.

"Here, Lindsay," her teacher said. "You see for yourself."

Patsy's report was not in a blue cover and the words inside were not exactly the same as Lindsay's. It was the thread of the composition that echoed her own work, the resemblance striking, and Lindsay reddened as she turned the pages. Fumbling to explain herself, she could only say that she'd finished the report early, that it had sat in their shared locker for a number of days. Mrs. Chalmers gave a doubtful half-smile and patted Lindsay's hand, as if to say, *Remember, this is Patsy Burgess we're talking about.*

Outside, Lindsay saw Patsy waiting to board her bus at the turnaround.

"You could have written about anything," Lindsay said, thinking of the Stamp Act and the Boston Tea Party.

Patsy smiled, showing an irregular line of teeth that in a few years would require extensive orthodontia.

"You heard what Teacher said," Patsy told her. "*You* have to do it again." She turned and climbed the steps of the bus and Lindsay watched it pull away and down the street. Her eyes smarted. It stuck her like a straight pin, not only the obvious fact of the theft, but also Patsy's smug certainty about their respective places in the world.

At home that afternoon, she tearfully recounted the story to her mother, who Lindsay hoped would set the teacher right. Her mother had witnessed her bent over the report; she could explain to Mrs. Chalmers what had happened. When Lindsay told the last of it, her mother only stared at her, stony as ever. And later: her father. At dinner Lindsay repeated it all and he listened, a fork suspended in midair. It seemed to Lindsay he was recognizing the shape of her injury, that it might have been a thing he'd understood in his life, too. But his expression shifted, as if he were gauging just how much of him it would take to defend Lindsay, his fear and shyness eventually crossing his face. He sighed. "I'm afraid you'll have to write the composition again, Linseed," he said, using his pet name for her.

It was an age-old memory but now, in the quarters of the tatty Pullman compartment, Lindsay experienced again the triple pinch of that day, of Patsy Burgess's theft, of her teacher and her parents. She could not see the woman with the cat-eye glasses from the *Cascade* treating her little girl in such manner and was surprised, after all these years, to find her eyes swimming.

It was sometime in the hours of night—Lindsay's watch had wound down. She thought of the story she'd told Atlee back on the *Empire Builder*, of Ed and the stolen kiss. Somebody had dragged the little man off before the police showed up. Whit—and Lindsay and the rest of the timber crew—had remained up at the bar, a dishtowel containing ice wrapped around the hand that had flattened Ed's nose, a drink in the other. The officers questioned Whit gingerly, as if they, too, were afraid of him. "I know what you boys want to know," he'd told the peace officers finally. "The why of it." He squinted an eye, as if taking aim. "The little bastard," he said, laughing. "I couldn't get a word in Ed-wise."

The train jostled over uneven rails. Lindsay smiled and imagined—her grip on the past gone slippery with fever— imagined what Whit would have done with Mrs. Chalmers, her parents and Patsy Burgess. And she saw it, fluttering like a strip of film on worn-out sprockets, the rather appealing picture of him decking the lot of them.

THE NEXT MORNING she did not take much note of the advancing rain heads. The flu weighed on her like an anchor, in her bones and other places. She dimly recalled Whit's letter, all the ground covered since she last capped her pen, since western Washington, but wasn't up to the task of continuing it.

Lindsay watched the weather front blow in, the storm clouds crowding out the blue until there was no blue left, everything below, the stubby high-plain country, rendered in grays, like an old-timey photograph. She could see cattle lying down in the fields, the Angus yearlings among the steers, their comical faces. She could see wind whipping down from the hills and through the valley. And running out ahead: tumbleweeds, what looked to be miles of them, like the phalanx of an army.

The front raced to broadside the train. It seemed the force of it might be strong enough to knock the line of cars off the tracks. When the winds slammed in, though, there was only the slightest bobble, the icy gusts finding every gap in the Pullman.

In the aftermath, flakes began to fall, a shock of white.

The snow still did not feel like luck as Whit had said, but it was riveting, how the storm boiled up on the horizon, like trouble, spinning over the bald plains, nothing to stop it.

In the corridor outside her compartment she heard the conductor conferring with the porter, later joined by the flagman, their voices low and earnest. Lindsay was in Wyoming now.

SHE MUST HAVE SLEPT.

It was late afternoon but could have been early morning, the blizzard's quality of half-light giving no indication. Out in the hallway, she asked the porter for the time. The porter appeared surprised to see her. Lindsay was wearing the same dress as the day before and maybe the one before that—it seemed like a week since she'd boarded the feeder line in Whitefish.

It was four-thirty.

The schedule had them in at Gatchell at three. She'd dozed clear through, and in realizing that her mind wheeled, then gave way to a cocktail of equal parts relief and disappointment. She'd hidden the visit to her parents behind the mystery of Gatchell and now there was only the sodden prospect of her family.

"What time did we make Gatchell?" she asked.

"Oh no, ma'am," the porter said softly. "We haven't reached Gatchell yet. We're running off schedule. It's the snows. We're only aiming to get the trains to the other end of the line. It miles and hours to Gatchell yet."

It was true: the train was crawling, grinding through the confusion of the storm. Lindsay thought it had been the thickness in her head, everything moving slower. The porter told her they'd come through the cars before Sheridan, warning of the severe weather ahead, in the Bighorns, suggesting the passengers wait it out in town, until conditions improved, and most had.

"I must have been asleep," she said and then, "I believe I've come down with something."

The porter smiled kindly. He had told Lindsay his name, back when she first boarded, Gregory or maybe George. "We're running a skeleton crew," he said. "I would think there is still something to eat in the lounge."

Lindsay did not feel hungry, had forgotten entirely about

food. She tried to think what she'd last consumed and the memory of the highballs returned, the spike of whisky repeating in her, a wave of nausea rising, then passing. There was a hole in the middle of her and it filled her up, a bubble, but maybe food could do some good.

The lounge car was empty except for Lindsay, a ghost train. The person manning the diner counter was off assisting the short-handed crew and when he returned to the car to fix sandwiches for them, he told her to help herself to whatever she could find and then was off again. Tea was all she could manage; it tasted like old socks steeping in a kettle. She must have looked a fright, the fever a fire inside her. Lindsay wondered if she was dying. This was sometimes how it happened, travelers stranded in a storm, too far from hospitals or country doctors. The idea did not particularly alarm her. Whit himself had nearly passed when he was a boy, a bout with scarlet fever.

The blizzard erased the high plains, only the snow which fell like streamers, the eerie sense that the train wasn't moving at all, that distance and time were frozen along with everything else. Once night dropped, a bank of floodlamps outside the domed roof were lit. She could see a shelf of snow extending in all directions, the occasional house half buried, havering in and out of the shimmer of white, like a mirage. The train shouldered heavily past a crossing and under a signal bridge, the semaphore blade on the top set in the diagonal position.

After Clearmont, the train gathered speed. It was still snowing but the tracks were somehow cleared of the weather, everything else covered save for the cross-hatching of rails and ties and an apron extending fifteen feet on either side. She could hear the crew calling, the conductor barking into the radio, conferring with the engineer or the next town down the line.

When the train began its climb into the Bighorns, it took miles for Lindsay to realize it—there was no horizon to mark up or down. And then more miles to catch the snow-fighting train ahead on the tracks. What she saw at first was a plume of white, like a fountain that appeared to issue not from the sky but the ground.

Then it came clearer. The snow train. At its nose was a steam engine equipped with a rotary blade, and this was bucking the snow, sending it into the air. Behind the engine, a crew car and then a steam locomotive, then a car with spreader wings which plowed a wider channel on either side of the tracks, along the right-of-way, pushing off not only snow but branches and downed trees. Last, a piece of rolling stock that cleared the flange-ways on the tracks.

Into the night she watched the activity of the snow train up ahead. At various times, men with picks and shovels would jump from the front, hack at a stubborn patch of ice, then clamber aboard the last car like hobos. Another crewman sometimes hung off the rear, signaling the engineer in Lindsay's train with a lantern.

Lindsay did not know if she'd ever seen anything quite so beautiful, the vision of the shower of snow, like stars being shot into a black sky. She was not one to be impressed with the hard labor of men and equipment, but the spectacle of the train cutting snow moved her.

And then morning and in the light of the hour Lindsay understood the punch of the storm. The train was in the mountains. On both sides of the tracks along the right-of-way, the wall of cleared snow reached almost up to the nest of the domeliner. In the distance she could see peaks, but mostly snow, that on the ground and the rest which continued to fall.

The train passed under another signal bridge, the crosspiece bearded in white, the semaphore blade at the top thrust outward, dead level. A few miles on, the vestiges of town, a few houses deep in the cotton of drifts, then more and then the modest parade square on main. Up ahead, off the rear of the snow train a crewman hung, swinging a lantern above his head, the groan of the passenger train coming to a halt, Lindsay pitching forward.

Men shouted from one train to the other, exclaiming something about the wheel-slip control. Shortly, the porter she'd talked with yesterday came into the car. They were stopping here, he told her. The snow was too high, the crew train unable to buck the drifts any further. Out on the main, she could see a plow, its pineapple-yellow light spinning, and behind it, an empty school bus coming to meet the train at the station. She could take one bag with her, the porter said, and leave the rest behind on the train, until they could resume again, until the storm finally blew out. The school bus would ferry the few who had failed to get off the train to accommodations in town.

She shivered, the sickness making itself known to her once more. It had been held at bay for the witchy hours of night, during the snow train's climb into the hills, as if she'd been able to stay a number of feet in front of it and only now that the train had stopped was it able to catch up. Lindsay walked uncertainly back to her Pullman. She threw together what she could in a small bag, taking the letter she'd begun back on the *Cascade* along with her, her crowded script like an artifact from an earlier time.

It was out on the station platform that she saw the painted sign and with that, the echo of Whit's words ringing in her ears like prophecy, the flight of chance that had worked to bring her to this spot. *Snow was luck.*

This was Gatchell. This was where Whit had run.

THE OCCIDENTAL HAD BEEN A PLACE, once, back when it could count on rail travel, not the few stragglers who crossed its threshold these days. It was coasting on whatever glamour still clung to its name. The lobby furnishings spoke of those times, the couches nearly the size of buffalo.

Lindsay dispatched the bellboy to the local drugstore to purchase whatever remedies could be had. She remained in her room, in the four-poster bed. There was the luxury of a bath, of which she availed herself. Food was left outside her door on a tray and it mostly went uneaten. Sometime during her stay, the house doctor was called upon and he thumped her chest and listened, held a flashlight and peered gravely into her mouth and nose and eyes. He looked like a cowboy, his mustache and the hat. Lindsay couldn't believe he was a bona fide doctor, not the people-seeing variety, but maybe horses and cattle.

It was the influenza, he informed her. Nothing to worry about, the medications that were available now. But it would have to run its course. She had a respiratory infection and the fever, one hundred and three degrees, he said, shaking out the thermometer.

"I'm booked on a train to back east," Lindsay told the doctor and showed him the waybill, as if that carried some authority with the sickness.

"You wouldn't be going anywhere even if you were in the pink," he told her. "We're still digging ourselves out from the storm." He nodded at the window. "Won't be a train for a number of days yet. You're lucky, getting sick when you did. You can take some consolation in that."

After he left, Lindsay wondered if maybe he was the medic called in for Whit, back when they found him. She'd read it had been in a sheep-shearing shed. He'd been missing for days.

Her side hurt from the shot that the doctor administered. She sat in a chair by the window and surveyed Gatchell. She could see from one end of main to the other. There was a saloon called the Century Club and another, the Green Room. There was a western wear and inside, along one wall, a soda fountain counter. There was the drug and notions store where she'd sent the bellboy. City hall. A library. The railroad depot.

A post office. With the snow, it all looked like a quaint holiday scene from another time.

Lindsay swallowed her pills, remained abed, gave herself over to the influenza. She dispatched the bellboy again, this time to send a wire to her parents: *Delayed by flu and bad weather. Waiting it out in Wyoming. Will send word when situation changes.* She thought again of her letter to Whit, the flood of words she'd found on the first days of the trip, and now all she had to say for herself were three clipped sentences.

One day she heard the faint blare of a brass band. It was Veterans Day, the parade. She watched the slow processional coming up main, the old soldiers staggering through the drifts like the still-walking wounded. It was possible a number of them knew Whit, used to gather with him at one of the saloons to trade stories, the fraternity of men and bullets. The thought occurred to Lindsay that Whit's widow might be among the throng gathered in the snow. She studied the faces. A high school girl read an essay from the bandstand. The women in the crowd were old, not how Lindsay envisioned the second wife. There was no reason to expect she still lived here. It had been a number of years and there was the stain of bad memory that would never wash out.

And this was Gatchell and it told Lindsay nothing.

THEN ANOTHER BLIZZARD HIT.

From the window it appeared that the town was still struggling with the press of the first snows, like a wind-up toy cranking down. The later storm stemmed from upslope conditions, confined largely to the Bighorns, and stole in after dark. By morning, Gatchell might never have existed at all.

Sometime before noon, the civil defense siren rang out. Not long after, the power went, the high-ceilinged plaster rooms of the Occidental cooling rapidly. The staff came through, knocking on the doors of the few lodgers. They were being moved to the Odd Fellows hall. There was heat there, a generator. Red Cross had donated blankets and beds.

"But I'm sick," Lindsay said.

The desk clerk groped for an answer but said nothing.

The IOOF hall proved worse than she'd anticipated. It smelled of men, of sweat and liquor. The walls were dark-paneled and there was the constant apiarian buzz of the generator. Rows of cots were arrayed in a large chamber that might have been a ballroom. It reminded Lindsay of barracks or a gypsy village. Children raced over the plank wood flooring, playing tag, shrieking, while adults stared at the whitewashed gloom outside.

The idea of sleeping in such arrangements, the muffled coughs and snores and distress of little ones waking to discover they'd wet the bedding—it was beyond Lindsay. She was mad at Whit. She sat on her small bag like an immigrant. And she was mad, her anger thorny and sharp, the injustice of his running off slapping her anew, like a delayed punchline. It took all she had not to cry. He had run and she'd followed in her own fashion, only wishing to get a handle on where he'd gone, what might have happened to him, and this was where it had all gotten her.

Lindsay had felt alone before but this was different. She glanced around at the townsfolk, everyone full to brimming with their own worries. Who might take care of her? She seemed as helpless as her parents, and the need for people—not just to chase loneliness but for actual survival—stuck in her throat like a chicken bone.

Perhaps the feeder line was running again, the miracle of the snow-fighting train able to buck the giant drifts. Lindsay found a pay telephone, the subsequent call confirming it would be days or more.

She sat on the stool in the booth, staring at the Gatchell phone book, scarcely thicker than a finger. She riffled the pages, opened it, curiosity leading her on a leash. She searched whether it still contained Whit's name, *her* name, and what she found was only one listing along with the initial A.

Lindsay dialed the number. It could be a distant cousin, she told herself, or just blind coincidence. With the dispiriting prospect of waiting out the storm at the hall, she was ready to try anything.

A woman answered.

"This might be hard to explain," Lindsay said.

"Yes?" the woman said cautiously.

"I'm Whit's wife," Lindsay told her.

Then silence: only the poor connection, crackling like fire.

"There must be a mistake," the woman said at last. "I was his wife."

"Well, I was the first one."

. . .

LINDSAY KNEW NOTHING OF ALEX, only the fact of her, invisible as a force of physics.

Whit had attended a symposium of writers and artists up in Washington, in Port Townsend—that was where it started with her, over the course of the several weeks that the conference lasted. Lindsay had stayed at home with the dogs.

He returned but only briefly, filled with a tenderness that Lindsay wanted to believe might be love, and she allowed the prospect to carry her like a kite. Perhaps they had weathered the worst. But, too, he had a look to him that she couldn't place, of a man arriving at a destination, and she waited for Whit to tell her what it was although he never did. There was only a letter that said what it had to say and that was all. *This is no way to leave you,* he'd written, *running off like an animal. But it is the only way that I can.* He had met someone else. He would not fight any matter of property or chattel.

And that was the last of him.

The fact he could surrender it all so readily, wanting nothing of the life they'd made—that was almost worse than the infidelity or the subsequent divorce. Lindsay's letters began then. There were still things that needed to be said, or at least aired, the whole business such a woefully undertold story, the ending he left her with, not an ending at all really.

She lacked the nerve to send the letters, didn't have any address for him anyway, and none of the missives ever traveled farther than the back of her desk drawer. It seemed appropriate even so. Whit had come at the world with words. That was what he had—words and spleen and energy—and in the end, words were all Lindsay had left. And where did they take her? She could only get so close and then no closer.

Waiting now for Alex in the cavernous vestibule of the IOOF hall, the hammer of a steam radiator keeping erratic time, Lindsay thought not of his leaving but instead of the sad last months with Whit before the conference, running through once again all the things she might have done to prevent what took root there.

The fight had not exactly gone out of him, the wonderful and furious energy. It got turned inward, against himself, and in time it grew to include Lindsay as well. He'd lost something or maybe it was the opposite, that he lacked some vital mechanism, like an engine firing on too few cylinders.

"I can help you," she had promised him but she did nothing more than hope for the best, no different from what she always did. Lindsay could sense more was required of her, however, more than just hope, though she had no idea what that might be.

She ached for the force to change things, all her life wanted that. It had been enough being with Whit, so close to his indomitable will, as if it were hers, too, there was so much of it. But in the shadow of his foundering, she recognized once again the limited shape of who she was and would ever be.

He'd taken to wandering the property nights, like a sleepwalker, though it was not the peace of slumber but drink.

Lindsay would wake in bed alone, set off to find him, fearing the worst, the lantern casting a faltering beam, the blot of the towering redwoods assuming the dark and wicked forms of childhood bugaboos. She would find him in the meadow or at a massive stump at the edge of woods or by the mossy creek-bank. When she roused him, he would talk a string of whisky gibberish, a haunting, impenetrable tongue that Lindsay could not decode. She believed he might be speaking an inner language, that perhaps Whit was communicating some secret antidote. And Lindsay strained to hear his words, the odd glottal syllables climbing in the air, through the overhang of trees and into the Bible-black night.

One night she'd waited to go after him. They had fought bitterly, his stinging accusations, some real, others imagined. Her jaw still pulsed from where he'd punched her. He was at the edge of the meadow before it fell away into bramble and the slough. When he spoke, she expected to hear his strange tongue.

"I thought you were Doris," he said calmly, her mother's name. Whit laughed softly. "I thought you were Doris."

Her mother was ugly but had been pretty once. Lindsay had seen the photos, though she never quite believed the fact until then, that implacable and remote woman, life's many disappointments having rotted her like a fungus. It seemed impossible that something like love might ever have existed in her, unseen yet beating, but maybe. And it struck Lindsay then harder than any blow, the gulf between people. One knew only so much and the rest had to be taken on faith, such an inadequate and gauzy fabric. That she could stand by and venture nothing to Whit except for toothless hope—it must have seemed permission to him, the license to fall as far as he wished.

"You will miss me when I'm gone," Whit said to her and she thought he meant the few weeks he would be away at the conference, though he'd been raising the threat even back then, of taking up his hand against himself. They were only a few feet apart, the tufted stalks of pampas grass wavering in a breeze. It could as well have been miles.

OUT THE FOGGED WINDOW of the IOOF vestibule Lindsay could see a plow, a hillbilly truck, actually, a cornbinder fitted with a blade that parted the drifts into twin rooster tails of snow, and following close behind, a rusted-out Pontiac sedan. Lindsay tugged her new hat lower across her brow, hoping she didn't look as foolish as she felt.

A little woman stepped out from the Pontiac wearing an overcoat several sizes too large and Lindsay thought at first she might be a child. The woman yelled something to the driver of the plow, then proceeded up the walkway, the brick steps and then inside.

"You must be Lindsay," she said. Alex was blond and attractive, in a furry sort of way, had a low voice, like Lindsay, odd that she'd not taken note of that during the phone call.

There was no time for small talk, the curtain of flakes reducing visibility to practically nothing. Alex was all business, hefting the bag over Lindsay's protest. "You're sick," she said. "Please, let me do it." And then they were off, following the plow's spray.

Alex lived several miles outside of town. The power was still running, she told Lindsay, but who knew for how long. They talked for a time about the vagaries of weather and when that petered out they rode in silence. Even with the neighbor out front with the plow, it seemed to take all their attention to keep the Pontiac on the icy pavement. Alex drove uncomfortably, as if she were sitting atop an orange crate, too heavy on all the pedals, working the shifter like a one-armed bandit, and Lindsay thought with a degree of satisfaction that it must have driven Whit near crazy.

Once free of town, it was the wavy expanse of grazing country again. Lindsay could not fathom what drew them here. Whit always used to joke that he needed to live near the sea, that he got *landsick* otherwise.

The influenza suddenly caught up with her again, fogging her head, all the legs of the trip seeming to run to this very spot. Before boarding the *Cascade* she'd not thought of Whit with such intensity for the longest time. She'd moved on, had stayed at the house in the woods, but otherwise had moved on. If she'd thought of him at all it was late afternoon, the hour he used to return from his writing shack, battered by the rigors of writing or perhaps not writing, ready for the first of many whiskies. These days Lindsay watched the news at that hour, on the console she allowed the eager salesman at the appliance store in town to peddle her, spectral images in a rice of static, a novelty that she couldn't ever see rivaling radio.

This Alex was saying something to her now. Along the road were high gates to ranch property, driveways leading past stock tanks to solitary houses in the distance. With her stuffed ears, all Lindsay could hear was that song that the engineer fellow from the *Empire Builder* had whistled. She could recall the melody, a Tommy Dorsey tune.

Alex's face screwed with concern. Such a birdlike creature! Lindsay pegged her as roughly the same age as herself. Neither of them looked their years, could have passed for much younger women. She watched Alex speaking to her, a mouth filled with so many teeth it reminded Lindsay of a piano. She was saying something, reaching over, shaking Lindsay's arm.

"Yes," Lindsay said sweetly to whatever Alex wanted to know. She smiled reassuringly. "Yes." The snow was really quite beautiful, swirling so wildly it could have been falling *up*. It reminded her of when she first spotted the snow train. She would have to tell Alex about that.

The neighbor piloting the plow beeped his horn, waved an arm out the window, and turned into a drive with a sign touting sporting clays and game bird hunting. Alex continued down the road, presently pulling along a red clapboard house, a stand of thin, insubstantial trees surrounding the structure, little more than saplings, nothing like the sequoias back home.

Alex was saying something else now. Even with the racket of the Pontiac mercifully shut off, Lindsay couldn't hear. And then she was in a room with cream walls the color of a paper lantern, a quilt with a folk hexagonal design pulled tight to her chest, a room that seemed to smell like Whit.

AFTER TEN MORE HOURS the fierce weather abated. In the lashing wind that followed, it might as well have been snowing, the white from the drifts which continued to blow. It reminded Lindsay of feathers, a shower of eider.

For the most part, the world on the other side of the crystal-rimmed window went unobserved. It seemed she had been sick not just days but years, and Lindsay faced the possibility of death with equanimity—a good soldier her father would have said—the thought occurring to her that passing was more a burden for the living than the dying. She considered those who might miss her, a slim list, but no matter. She luxuriated in this new sense of herself and when the flu was eventually chased two days on, she would feel as silly as a teenager, glad to let the morbid thoughts go along with the chills and night sweats.

Until then, Alex was a dim presence, peeking in the room, leaving broth on a table. Occasionally, Lindsay would hear a radio from somewhere in the house and Alex talking softly to herself or perhaps to a dog. Once Lindsay believed she glimpsed Alex in a ridiculously pink housecoat, but maybe not.

On the last night before the sickness retreated she dreamed that her body temperature had dropped to seventy-seven degrees and her skin had turned to armor, a troubling image that woke her and it was hours until she could bob back to sleep. And then it was morning and Lindsay was better, still a bit weak but out of the woods. It was a brilliant day, a glare of arctic white padding the ground. The sky was so clear it surprised her, the blue filling all of it, even to the north, from where the storm had blown in, replacing the smudge of dark nimbus that Lindsay had taken as a permanent fixture here on the high plains, like an imperfection.

"I FEEL BETTER," Lindsay told Alex downstairs at breakfast, which amounted to a fairly spartan spread: toast and jam, tea, juice. Lindsay was famished and helped herself to everything. For her part, Alex didn't eat. Lindsay was not a big woman but she felt oafish in comparison. She imagined Alex stealing furtive bites on the run, when nobody was watching.

"Yes," Alex said, "I was worried. I'm glad."

"I am so sorry for intruding on you this way," Lindsay said. "It was panic, I suppose. The prospect of bunking in that drafty hall." She shook her head at the idea.

"You were right to call," Alex assured her, though something in her face made Lindsay doubt this, a wariness, nothing in particular, but there.

Lindsay looked at the frozen expanse framed by the window. If anything, the drifts showed the country better, softened it up. Even so she couldn't find much to recommend it. Far off, across an ocean of white, the shapes of barns and outbuildings. A person could see for miles out here, trouble announcing itself long before it lit.

"I phoned earlier about the train," Alex said.

"Oh, yes. I'd nearly forgotten about the schedule in all the excitement."

"They think the line will be running in two days."

"Good news," Lindsay said brightly.

Alex's face closed up a little again. "Of course, you are welcome to stay. I can understand if you're not quite up to the idea of travel yet."

"I'm sure that will be fine," Lindsay told her. "Two days' time."

A dog entered the kitchen, a black-and-white that offered Lindsay its wet snout, then lay at her feet and chewed a front leg like it was a corncob.

"Good," Alex said, her face relaxing now that that was settled. "I must get to work. I hope you don't feel abandoned."

Lindsay waved off any concern. "I'll be fine."

"There are magazines and the radio, if you wish." Alex glanced around to see if she was omitting anything. "We'll talk later. I look forward to it." She set off for a room in the back of the house that she called her studio.

That was right: Alex was an artist of some stripe. Lindsay knew that, one of the few things she did know. After Whit ran off she'd told the few people who asked that Alex fashioned trinkets that she sold to the tourists, although that was just anger talking. In truth, Lindsay had no idea.

She roamed the house, silky spiderwebs at the top corners

of the doorways, a colony of box-elder bugs living under the sink in the bathroom. Lindsay peeked into the refrigerator and the pantry, finding not much, tins of tomato soup and various jars of nuts, not the bounty a person should lay in during storm season, out here on the frontier. She looked for evidence of Whit and there was hardly any, not even copies of his books on the shelf, no snapshots taken after he left her, only the author photo from the jacket of *Night Voyage* in a dusty frame sitting on the mantel in the living room; aside from that, nothing that said he'd lived here.

It was only when she returned to the room with the paper-lantern-colored walls that Lindsay realized she'd ridden out the influenza in Whit's writing study. His rickety black Royal typewriter sat squarely at attention, the stacks of white bond paper he was so persnickety about, a leather-bound *Merriam-Webster's*, the binding worse for wear.

Lindsay sat behind the Royal, her fingers resting on the keys. Her foot nudged something under the writing table: a file box. She expected to find old manuscripts inside, pages yellowed and ink faded. But it wasn't that. The pages were of a more recent vintage, three years maybe, from back when Whit was still alive, and she pulled them out for closer inspection. It was work she had never seen before, obviously from his hand, the hanging cap T of the Royal that she recognized. He'd published nothing after leaving her, not even posthumously, when interest in his work skyrocketed. He'd been all used up, nothing left—that was the conventional wisdom. As hard as it was to believe, Lindsay ultimately accepted it as fact.

She trembled as she read the pages, difficult to determine what exactly they were, the characters from a long-ago time and place. A bit appeared to be notes, other parts pieced together in what suggested a letter.

Then Lindsay caught the thread of it and it was unlike anything she'd read from Whit before. They were stories that hadn't yet been stitched to form a whole. The people lived in sod houses with dirt floors, a community of farmers isolated from the rest of the world, a world that was its own.

Even in its rough state, the manuscript thrilled Lindsay. It was lovely, the hum and glow of his sentences. For the first time in a long while, the memories were good. The days of Whit emerging triumphant from his writing shack. "You're going to have to hose me off, dear," he would joke, the spark of his fire evident all the way through him. Their nights of playing cribbage over the kitchen table, eating late or not at all, Whit holding forth, gripped in his own power. The glorious days when words had been enough.

It was dark outside when Lindsay glanced up from the table. From downstairs, Alex in the kitchen, the sound of supper underway.

THE MEAL WAS AN UNREMARKABLE STEW but Lindsay had no complaint. She was still held in the spell of the pages, their rough magic flushing her with the tincture of something like love, maybe not love exactly, but a reclamation of a tiny piece of what was once hers.

The talk was awkward, the same circling that marked breakfast, Alex speaking carefully, repeating many of the questions that Lindsay posed, as if she needed to back up, to gather herself before answering. It turned out they were both younger siblings and this was a starting point.

"Yes," Alex said. "The tyranny of older sisters. It's the same everywhere, isn't it?"

In the corner of the room, a Franklin woodstove ticked. Nearby, the dog lay on the brick hearthway, its coat bulky as a ski sweater.

"So I take it you're from this area?" Lindsay asked, gently probing, the idea occurring to her that Whit and Alex might have decided to call this windswept speck on the map home for no better reason than that.

No, that wasn't the case, Alex told her. "My people are from Nebraska and Minnesota," she said.

"I myself," Lindsay said, "am on my way to visit my folks back east. The Hudson Valley." She pulled a face to show her displeasure and when Alex smiled, Lindsay understood that she'd not yet stated what had brought her to Wyoming, understood as well that that might explain some of the reticence. It was a nice smile, generous and somewhat sly; Alex could stand to use it more often, was all.

After dinner, they had tea in the living room. Lindsay hoped things were opening up. She longed to ask about the secret pages upstairs in Whit's study, and then all the other questions, a matter of drawing Alex out, she believed, of winning her over, no reason they couldn't be friends.

Whit's photo from *Night Voyage* stared at her from the mantel and Lindsay gestured toward it. "I saw a man reading that book on the Great Northern. I should be accustomed to it now. But it's still strange, seeing that familiar face."

Alex nodded.

And with that small acknowledgment, Lindsay felt free to open the door to the subject, if only a crack. "Speaking of childhoods," she said. "Before. At dinner, I mean. I never tired of hearing about Whit's. The stories." There was the chum nicknamed Etiquette Andy who cussed like a stevedore in the schoolyard but had impeccable manners around grown-ups.

"I'd heard of him," Alex said, and asked if Lindsay knew the one about the imp who convinced Whit to swallow wet cement.

"Tommy Stokes," Lindsay said.

"Yes," Alex echoed. She referred to Whit as Shelby, by his last name, which struck Lindsay as cheeky. At least they were talking more freely now.

"I've felt him these past few days," Alex said. She looked away, then back to Lindsay. "More than usual. Your flu reminded me. His bout with scarlet fever."

"It did me, too," Lindsay said. "I wasn't nearly as ill. Those were the days before sulfa drugs, of course. I always suspected maybe it wasn't quite as bleak a situation as he'd painted. Whit was always one for self-dramatization."

They sat and said nothing for a time. Lindsay could see whatever warmth she'd managed to elicit from Alex cooling along with the tea. But she was getting closer to what she wanted to know. The pages upstairs were part of it and the rest—that was what she would find out.

"There was always something of the child in him," Lindsay continued. "The adult never firmly taking root." She chuckled to herself. "I could tell you stories," she said and then she did, launching into the time at the roadhouse by the Eel, the tiny logger Ed and his ill-advised kiss. It was not quite the same as aboard the *Empire Builder*, this version carrying the air of swapping secrets with a confederate.

"I'm not one to endorse violence," Lindsay said at the end, after Whit had socked Ed clear over the bartop. "But sometimes it takes a man to remind you that you're a woman." She smiled as if the small victory was not only hers but Alex's, too: this was the person they married, reckless and unbroken. And Lindsay waited expectantly when she was done. Alex no doubt could tell her own tales.

There was only the snuffling of the dog inspecting its nether areas, the pop of fire in the kitchen woodstove.

"That's hard for me to imagine," Alex said finally, each word coming slowly. "He didn't drink during my time with him."

Lindsay sensed blood rising in her face. It was not the news that Whit had given up whisky; he'd always vowed one day to do so. It was how easily this little woman trumped her story. Alex owned the final word on him. It didn't matter that Lindsay had spent more years with Whit. Alex was with him at the end.

The tea was cold by now. Lindsay made a show of sipping it anyway. She had nothing else to say.

It was Alex who spoke next. "Would you care to see some of my work?" she asked shyly and Lindsay said, why yes, she would.

The studio was a converted storage room off the breeze-way at the back of the house, a deep laundry sink, jugs of chemicals on shelves. Alex explained that she worked with glass-plate negatives from the century before. She hefted a boxy portrait camera to show Lindsay, its leather bellows extending like an elephant's trunk. "This is the beast," she said. "In many respects, not altogether different from a Brownie." It was a matter of exposing the antique glass plates to light, using a contact printer to create a photograph the same size as the negative. "There's more to it than that, but that's the nut of it," Alex said.

She discussed all this without her usual reserve, her passion for the work obvious and a thing that Lindsay envied. Lindsay believed an artistic pulse beat inside her as well. After Whit ran off, she'd enrolled in the occasional art class at the community college and eventually swamped out his writing shack, enlisting the handyman from down the road to plug the mouse holes, install a proper roof, frame in additional windows, and it housed her many projects, her unfinished sketches, end tables earmarked for decoupage, a weather-beaten ukulele that couldn't hold a tuning, the sundry interests that won Lindsay's attention for a time only to get replaced by something else, all of it such a sham.

Alex's photographs were scenes from the Great Plains, pioneer families with faces set hard in determination, the privation of that life, men with odd wide-brimmed hats, women in bonnets, the land gray and unforgiving, each print a window onto another place, the shapes on the 8×10 exposures shimmering out of the smoke and haze of age. Some were portraits of ranch hands at work—branding and shearing and threshing crews. But it was the more domestic shots that struck Lindsay. A man with a chin-strap beard and his dour wife lifting a killed eagle, each gripping a wing. A Christmas scene around a spindly tree. A little girl clutching a doll, gazing into the camera with heartbreaking sorrow.

Lindsay had no words for their beauty, the salty severity, each photograph bearing a hint of Alex, not only because her hands had teased the images from the murk of chemicals, but because there was indeed *something* of her in the portraits, the faces that only told so much and nothing more.

"It's been a long day," Alex said softly.

Lindsay murmured, "I could view these all night long."

Alex cleared her throat. "I was thinking that if you're up to it, tomorrow we could take a walk in the snow. There are teepee rings. They're not terribly far."

"I would like that," Lindsay told her. "I would."

She retired to Whit's writing study for the evening, too weary to delve into any more of the manuscript. She lay in bed, surprised to discover anger welling inside her. For so long, Whit had been a volatile, yet known, quantity, his end a logical extension of the decline he'd begun with Lindsay. Now she wasn't so sure. The little of him that Alex had described sounded nothing like the man Lindsay had married. She wondered if he'd ever hit Alex and, with a pang of jealousy, decided he'd not. It rankled Lindsay that Alex's life with him seemed better than hers, or maybe not as bad. And that woman's damned guardedness: what was she protecting out here? Lindsay was practically family, for goodness sakes. Before falling asleep she repeated what she told herself more than once during the course of the day, that she was a guest in this house, Alex's house, and no matter how sourly matters sat with her, it ultimately wasn't her say.

I am getting better, Lindsay wrote the next morning in her letter to Whit. Her previous entry was from eastern Washington. *There are hawks spinning like lassos above the river,* she had written then. She tried to piece together that setting, but only a vague picture surfaced. That was eight days ago though it felt much longer, years and miles, an unbridgeable distance. *I am in Gatchell,* she added now. *In your house.*

She dressed in one of the two skirt and blouse combinations she'd brought in her small bag from the snow-buried train, and descended the stairs. A note on the kitchen table said that Alex was already at work and after lunch they could take their hike to the teepee rings. The dog beat its tail on the floor, then limped over. Lindsay fed it crusts of buttered toast.

"Do you remember Whit?" she asked the dog. The black-and-white cocked its head, waited for more toast.

Lindsay retreated upstairs, resumed reading the manuscript for the balance of the morning. This last part proved to be the most coherent yet, the footing steady, Whit getting his legs underneath him. A respected church elder dies and the men in town gather to select a new elder, a matter of writing initials on bits of paper and collecting them in a hat. Most of the assembled have earned the wisdom of years, the selfless truths that arise from seasons in the fields, countless sabbaths of prayerful worship. There is one fellow recently of majority, practically a boy but not a boy, a young man who accompanies his father to the selection. His father is widely venerated, an upright individual, but it is the son who has won the heart of the community. He is something of a prodigy, his serene grace, the wisdom of a young Solomon, and when the vote is tallied, his initials account for the lion's share. It is his father, however, who steps forward. They own the same initials, the same name, and though the truth of the selection is clear to everyone, it remains unspoken in the hall, not only for the ordained commandment of respecting one's forebear but the unwritten sin of a son preceding a father.

Lindsay heard the whir of a motor, probably an exhaust fan back in Alex's studio. Outside, the day was shaping up nicely, a replica of yesterday.

Only a few pages left.

After the church selection vote, the son is devastated, unable to square his 'opposing feelings, his love for his father, the longing to assume his own rightful place in the community. It's confounding: the infinitely fine shadings that separate purpose and ambition. In the end, he flees or that at least is the story told later by the townspeople. In truth, his hat is found floating in the river, the circle of its crown like a black sun in the water, the possibility of any other outcome unspoken, like the vote itself.

Lindsay sat back from the table. She did not know what to make of it, so different from anything she'd ever read from Whit, no dogsledding or tales from the hunt. There were the spare words he'd written and the rest that he did not, the hole between wide enough to drive a truck through.

ALEX BUNDLED LINDSAY in a long wool overcoat that Lindsay realized after a few moments had been Whit's, the familiar spiky smell of tobacco in its nap. Alex wore pants again, sensible given the weather, though it made her tomboyish.

The cold was stunning, its dryness scraping at Lindsay's throat and nasal passages like a fish scaler. They trudged single-file through the untracked drifts, Alex out front, breaking trail, Lindsay following, the steady chorus of their labored breathing. They headed in the direction of a large barn. Alex's house appeared small from this distance, not like a home at all, more a country schoolhouse. They angled off, crossed the road, then proceeded overland through the drifts, the land undulating with small hills, a few houses nestled along a drainage creek, roofs flocked with white.

They began a slow ascent up a knobby hill, tough going for Lindsay, weak yet from the influenza, her stockinged legs cold but dry. "I'm fine," she told Alex during the climb, the rest of the way up tramping again in silence. Lindsay concentrated on the few square yards around her, the one-two rhythm of her marching feet, Alex out front, a watch cap pulled tight on her head, hair the color of broom straw.

From the ridgeline Lindsay could see the snaggled shapes of the Bighorns, an impressive sight. They paused to catch their breath. Just a bit more to go, Alex told her. Then off again, the hiking easier on the crest. They continued until they reached a drop-off where the shoulders of the valley came up to meet them. Down below, the county road bisected the snowfields, Alex's house small as a toy. From somewhere Lindsay heard the distant gargle of a motor, though no vehicle was in evidence. It was an enormous valley, hard to picture that in eight months' time the land would be remade, waving in a thick mane of alfalfa, the high plains peppered with the black of Angus stock. This was the time of year that it happened—December actually. The land must have been locked in the ice chest of winter then, too. Lindsay thought about the story she'd read earlier, imagined Whit going off after typing the last of it, going into afternoon, night already spreading across the sky. A tidy account, although she knew in her bones that probably wasn't it.

"The rings are circles of stones," Alex explained. "Under the snow."

"What are those?" Lindsay asked, pointing to the string of buildings in the far-off. She'd hoped that the view from the ridgeline might tell her more, had the improbable notion that she at least might see teepees up here.

"Wintering sheds for the cattle," Alex answered.

Farther afield, a smaller shape, a solitary building, its walls encased in an outer wall of snow. Lindsay remembered the ranch hands from the daguerreotypes that Alex had shown her last night, the sheep-shearing crews.

"What about that building?" she said. "Out there."

A wind crowded the valley, the sound of it like a holler, then it blew out and toward the Bighorns.

"Isn't that a sheep-shearing shed?" Lindsay pressed.

Alex gazed off in the other direction, toward her house and the road that led to Gatchell.

Lindsay wanted to shake the woman. *Just answer the question.* She'd had enough of this secretiveness or whatever it was. How much was she supposed to put up with? She'd been the injured party, too. This woman, after all, had stolen her husband.

"What happened to him?" Lindsay said abruptly.

"What happened to Shelby?" Alex repeated softly, still staring off, as if waiting on somebody below to drive up the road and take her away from this.

"Why do you do that?" Lindsay said.

"Do what?"

"Call him Shelby. His name was Whit."

"It was Shelby, too."

The anger was on Lindsay now. It had been there all along, not only since reaching Gatchell, but before. It was on her now, her arm already swinging in Whit's longcoat before she could stop it. She more cuffed Alex across her head than punched her, knocking the smaller woman into the snow, the momentum pitching Lindsay forward on top of her. She couldn't determine whether Alex was fighting her off or actually fighting back, the two of them wrestling in the deep bank. Lindsay believed she heard the wind again, angry now, but it was her own voice, strangled, choking with fury. What the hike and sickness hadn't taken out of her, the first flurry of blows did. Alex was smaller but she had the advantage now. Lindsay braced herself. Alex only staggered to her feet, stood over Lindsay, hair flying and electric.

"Why did you come here?" Alex sputtered. "What did you think you would find?" She didn't wait for an answer, the crunch of her boots breaking snow. Then Alex sideslipping down the hill and away. Lindsay remained where she lay. The sky was cast in a color so deep it couldn't possibly have a name. She could stay here, let night drop over, sleep in this bed of ice. Dying wasn't the hardest thing in the world.

After a while, Lindsay worked her way onto her knees and then up. Their impression in the white, from where they had rolled around, looked like the snow angels she and her sister used to make when they were children, little girls waving arms and legs on the ground, gazing toward heaven.

WHEN LINDSAY TRAMPED BACK to the red house it was the last of afternoon. Nobody home. She felt like a drink in the worst way and rooted around in the kitchen but came up empty, then holed up in her room.

Now it was night and she couldn't sleep. Tomorrow she would board the feeder line and continue on her way; for the moment that offered little solace. She was still mad, mostly at herself. She stared up at the ceiling. Too antsy to stay abed, she swung her legs out, stood, went into the hallway.

A dark shape coalesced down at the end of the hall. The dog, that poor arthritic creature. Lindsay tiptoed over, remembering fondly the companionship of her own dogs over the years. She could pass the hours till morning, soothed by its forgiving eyes.

Nearing it, Lindsay saw it wasn't the dog at all. It was Alex.

"I feel so horrible," Lindsay whispered.

"I do also," Alex said.

"I just couldn't stay in that room any longer."

"Come here," Alex said, grasping Lindsay's arm, leading her to the room at the end of the hall, inside, and into the bed. Lindsay's eyes were suddenly flushed with tears, for simple kindnesses, for herself, for reasons that reached all the way back, life's countless knocks and injuries. Alex rubbed Lindsay's shoulder, whispered words that sounded faintly Germanic, and this was how she fell asleep.

She woke once during the night, their arms and legs atangle in the bedding. Lindsay shifted to free herself and Alex stirred, her eyes still closed. Their faces were inches apart but the kiss that followed seemed to travel across a great expanse. A tooth of Lindsay's had come loose in the tussle but she held on to Alex and the kiss, could feel the points of Alex's breasts through her nightshirt. And she held on, not knowing if Alex was even awake. It lasted as long as Lindsay needed.

Then somehow it was morning again, the other side of the bed empty.

THERE WAS STILL TIME BEFORE THE TRAIN, which would depart just before noon. They sat in the living room and for once Alex directed the conversation.

"My grandfather only took a train ride once in his life," she said. "Actually never. When he died. Bringing the coffin from Minnesota to Nebraska." They were General Conference Mennonites. She told Lindsay something of that life, the hymn-singing, the austerity of day-to-day existence, a life apart. "His name was Menno," Alex said.

Lindsay listened, unsure why Alex was telling her this. *We all have families*, she seemed to be saying. *We all come from somewhere.* Perhaps Alex felt as isolated here as her relations did from the rest of their world. Whit had pulled her to a place out on the frontier, then left her there.

"Those photos," Lindsay said.

"My relatives," Alex told her. "My grandfather was the one with the eagle."

"Why stay here?"

"A person has to live somewhere."

A clock on the mantel bonged, marking the hour.

"I miss him," Lindsay said. "The way he smelled. I used to tell myself that he was away on a trip. After he left. He was gone but he might come back. It had never been quite real. But now here we are."

"Here we are," Alex said. She brushed the fabric on a sofa cushion, then met Lindsay's eyes. "It was wonderful, the weeks of that conference. Port Townsend. But that wasn't the real world, was it? A community of artists. We thought we could just live on that, that that could be enough. And it *was* glorious for a while, running away to here. We thought we could build something of our own. But the world has a way of finding you."

Lindsay understood something of this. It could have been anywhere. "You don't have to tell me this," she said.

They sat in the living room, both, in their own way, pretty women.

"I guess we won't be having children," Lindsay said.

"At least not together," Alex said and laughed. She really did have a nice smile.

Time to go. Lindsay climbed the stairs to the study to collect her bag. She shoved the file box under the writing table where she'd found it. It was Alex's world he'd been writing about, the long-ago people in their simple dress and ways. Or maybe not. In the end, there was only what Lindsay knew and all that she didn't. She knelt under the table, opened the box again. On the last of her letter to him she wrote the word *Goodbye* and slid the pages into the box.

FALL HAD BATTLED BACK AGAINST WINTER, the day warming, a squadron of clouds throwing shadows on the snowfields. Alex drove at a good clip into Gatchell, still herky-jerky on the pedals as the car bounced over the packed snow. Nearing town, the streets were plowed clean. Lindsay could see the clock tower of the town hall and the depot at the end of main. The road was indeed paved red, like the man on the *Empire Builder* had told her, the crushed clinker rock.

"I believe I'd like to walk from here," Lindsay said.

Alex braked. "Are you sure? I can drive you the rest of the way. I'd be happy to."

"I'm up to it," Lindsay told her.

The car rumbled in neutral.

Lindsay opened the door. "I can see why Whit—" she said, stopping herself, then bobbing her head at all she didn't say. "It's not hard to see why."

"I can see why with you, too," Alex said and then, "I could never talk to him about his writing. You could. He told me."

Lindsay allowed herself a small smile. This was hers. She had lost Whit twice but she still had this. "There were things I couldn't do for him, either," she confessed.

Alex's face gave way, all the strings going slack, the years of lugging doubt and guilt.

"We do what we can," Lindsay assured her, squeezing her hand.

Outside the car Lindsay could hear the activity of town, a vibration. She watched Alex pull the Pontiac into a wide U-turn, then gone. The Wyoming air tasted as fresh and clean as water. For a while, it was enough to stand there and simply take it in.

A few other travelers made their way to the depot. Up front of the feeder line, a team of locomotives snorted like a pair of rodeo bulls. The porter from a few days before greeted Lindsay outside her Pullman. His name was George, she remembered.

"How are you ma'am?" George asked.

"I'm feeling better," she told him, accepting his offer of a hand as she mounted the step stool into the train. And then, swinging her bag like a schoolgirl, she practically skipped up the aisle to her roomette. Lindsay would be foolish again, but never this young, and she would remember the moment—life picking itself up and moving on.

ACKNOWLEDGMENTS

"Betty Hutton" previously appeared in *Five Points* and "In the Snow Forest" in *Glimmer Train*. An excerpt from "Menno's Granddaughter" entitled "Cascade" appeared in *Open Spaces*.

The author would like to thank the following institutions and individuals: The Ucross Foundation. Greg Changnon, Tom Franklin, Peter Rock, Beth Ann Fennelly, Matthew Iribarne, Christine Hiebert, John Ristow, Kevin Schindler, Annie Callan, Suzanne Remington, Marianne Merola. And Gail Hochman.

A debt of gratitude is due the following texts: *The Klamath Knot* (Sierra Club Books) by David Rains Wallace, *Ice Fishing* (Countryman Press) by Jim Capossela, *The Body Language of Poker* (Lyle Stuart) by Mike Caro, *Classic American Streamliners* (MBI Publishing) by Mike Schafer and Joe Welsh, and *The American Railroad Passenger Car*, Vols. I and II (Johns Hopkins) by John H. White, Jr.